Whispering Angels

Christian fiction, Volume 2

Gregory Allen Parker

Published by Graywolf Press, 2024.

This is a work of fiction. Similarities to real people, places, or events are entirely coincidental.

WHISPERING ANGELS

First edition. August 3, 2024.

Copyright © 2024 Gregory Allen Parker.

ISBN: 979-8227139252

Written by Gregory Allen Parker.

Table of Contents

To all those who seek light in times of darkness, and to the whispering angels who guide us along the way. This book is dedicated to the resilient spirits who find strength in faith, love in community, and hope in the divine presence that surrounds us all. May you always hear the gentle whispers guiding you toward your true purpose.

Chapter 1: The Call to Faith

Introduction to the Protagonist

Sarah Langston sat by the window of her small apartment, staring blankly at the bustling street below. The world outside was alive with people going about their daily lives, but Sarah felt detached from it all. It had been six months since the accident, six months since her world had turned upside down. Her fiancé, Michael, had been taken from her in a tragic car accident, and since that day, Sarah had been struggling to find meaning in her life.

Once a vibrant and outgoing woman, Sarah now found solace in isolation. She rarely left her apartment except for work, and even there, she kept to herself. Her colleagues had stopped inviting her to social events, understanding her need for space, but the loneliness was beginning to consume her.

Faith had always been a part of Sarah's life, but in the wake of Michael's death, she found it increasingly difficult to believe in a higher power. How could a loving God allow such a tragedy? The question haunted her, and her once-steadfast faith wavered.

One dreary Saturday morning, as rain tapped softly against the windowpane, Sarah's thoughts were interrupted by the sound of her phone ringing. She glanced at the screen and saw the name "Grace" flashing. Grace Miller was an old friend from college, someone Sarah hadn't spoken to in years. Curiosity piqued, she answered the call.

"Hello, Sarah? It's Grace. How have you been?"

Grace's voice was warm and familiar, bringing a small smile to Sarah's face. "Hi, Grace. It's been a while. I'm... I'm hanging in there."

"I heard about Michael," Grace said gently. "I'm so sorry for your loss. I wish I had reached out sooner."

Sarah felt a lump form in her throat. "Thank you, Grace. It's been really hard."

"I can only imagine," Grace replied sympathetically. "Listen, I was thinking about you and wondered if you'd like to catch up sometime. Maybe grab a coffee?"

Sarah hesitated. The idea of socializing felt daunting, but a part of her yearned for connection. "Yeah, I think I'd like that."

"Great! How about tomorrow afternoon at The Java Bean on Fifth Street?"

"Sounds good. I'll see you then," Sarah agreed, feeling a flicker of hope.

Reconnecting with an Old Friend

THE NEXT DAY, SARAH made her way to The Java Bean, a quaint café she and Grace had frequented during their college years. The smell of freshly brewed coffee and the soft hum of conversation greeted her as she entered. She spotted Grace sitting at a corner table, waving enthusiastically.

"Sarah, over here!" Grace called out, her smile bright and inviting.

Sarah approached the table, feeling a mix of nervousness and anticipation. Grace stood up and enveloped her in a warm hug. "It's so good to see you, Sarah."

"You too, Grace," Sarah replied, returning the embrace.

They sat down and ordered their drinks, slipping into a comfortable conversation about their college days, reminiscing about old friends and shared experiences. It felt good to laugh again, even if only for a moment.

"So, what have you been up to all these years?" Sarah asked, genuinely curious.

Grace's eyes sparkled with excitement. "I've been pretty busy. I got married a couple of years ago, and I've been working as a youth counselor at a local church."

"A church?" Sarah repeated, her interest piqued. "I didn't know you were religious."

Grace nodded. "I found my faith a few years ago, and it's been an incredible journey. I've met some amazing people and experienced things that have truly changed my life."

Sarah's heart ached at the mention of faith. She wanted to believe again, to feel that sense of purpose and connection, but the pain of Michael's death still lingered. "I've been struggling with my faith lately," she admitted. "It's hard to believe in anything after losing Michael."

Grace reached across the table and took Sarah's hand. "I understand. Losing someone you love is one of the hardest things anyone can go through. But sometimes, faith can be a source of comfort and healing. Would you be interested in coming to church with me? No pressure, just a chance to see if it might help."

Sarah hesitated. The idea of going to church felt both foreign and intriguing. "I don't know, Grace. I'm not sure if I'm ready for that."

Grace squeezed her hand reassuringly. "Just think about it. No rush. I'm here for you, whatever you decide."

They continued their conversation, talking about lighter topics and sharing more memories. As they parted ways, Grace gave Sarah a hug and whispered, "You're not alone, Sarah. Remember that."

A Strange but Comforting Presence

THAT NIGHT, SARAH LAY in bed, her mind racing with thoughts of her conversation with Grace. The idea of finding comfort in faith was appealing, but she couldn't shake her doubts. She closed her eyes and tried to sleep, but a sense of restlessness kept her awake.

As she tossed and turned, she felt a strange but comforting presence in the room. It was as if someone was there with her, watching over her. The feeling was so strong that she sat up and looked around, but there was no one there.

Confused and a little frightened, Sarah lay back down, trying to calm her racing heart. The presence didn't go away; instead, it seemed to envelop her in a gentle embrace. She felt an inexplicable sense of peace wash over her, and for the first time in months, she fell into a deep, restful sleep.

The next morning, Sarah woke up feeling surprisingly refreshed. The memory of the comforting presence lingered, and she couldn't help but wonder if it had been a sign. She decided to give Grace's invitation some serious thought.

The First Step Towards Healing

THE FOLLOWING SUNDAY, Sarah found herself standing outside the church Grace had mentioned. The building was modest but inviting, with a small garden and a sign that read "Welcome to All." She took a deep breath and walked inside, her heart pounding with nerves.

Grace spotted her immediately and rushed over to greet her. "Sarah, you came! I'm so glad."

Sarah managed a small smile. "I figured I'd give it a try."

Grace led her to a pew near the front, and they sat down as the service began. The pastor, a kind-looking man named John, spoke about love, loss, and the power of faith to heal even the deepest wounds. His words resonated with Sarah, touching something deep within her.

As the service continued, Sarah felt the same comforting presence she had experienced the night before. It was as if someone was whispering words of encouragement and hope into her heart. She closed her eyes and let the feeling wash over her, tears streaming down her face.

After the service, Grace introduced Sarah to Pastor John. "This is my friend, Sarah. She's been through a lot recently."

Pastor John smiled warmly. "It's a pleasure to meet you, Sarah. I'm glad you decided to join us today."

"Thank you," Sarah replied, feeling a little overwhelmed. "I'm not sure what I believe anymore, but I felt something today, something... comforting."

"That's a good start," Pastor John said gently. "Faith is a journey, and it's okay to have doubts. What matters is that you're open to exploring it."

Grace gave Sarah a reassuring smile. "You don't have to figure everything out right now. Just take it one step at a time."

Sarah nodded, feeling a glimmer of hope for the first time in months. "Thank you, both of you. I'll keep coming, and see where this journey takes me."

Embracing the Journey

OVER THE NEXT FEW WEEKS, Sarah continued to attend church with Grace. Each service brought a new sense of peace and understanding. The comforting presence she felt grew stronger, guiding her through her doubts and fears.

One evening, after a particularly moving service, Sarah sat with Grace in the church garden, watching the sunset. "I've been feeling something, Grace. It's like there's someone watching over me, whispering words of comfort. Do you think it could be an angel?"

Grace smiled, her eyes filled with warmth. "I believe it could be, Sarah. Angels are often described as messengers of God, sent to guide and protect us. Maybe your angel is helping you find your way back to faith."

Sarah felt a sense of awe and gratitude. "I want to believe that. It feels so real, so... comforting."

Grace took Sarah's hand and gave it a gentle squeeze. "You're not alone, Sarah. Whether it's an angel or just the presence of God, you're being guided and protected. Trust in that, and let it lead you on this journey."

As the days turned into weeks, Sarah's faith began to blossom once more. She started volunteering at the church, finding joy in helping others and connecting with her community. The comforting presence remained with her, whispering words of encouragement and hope.

One evening, as Sarah sat in her apartment, journaling about her experiences, she felt a sudden urge to pray. She hadn't prayed in months, but the feeling was so strong that she couldn't ignore it. She knelt by her bed and bowed her head.

"Dear God," she whispered, her voice trembling. "Thank you for guiding me back to faith. I don't understand everything, and I still have doubts, but I trust that You're with me. Please continue to guide me and help me heal."

As she finished her prayer, a wave of peace washed over her. The comforting presence seemed to wrap around her like a warm embrace, and she

knew, deep in her heart, that she was on the right path.

Finding Community and Purpose

AS SARAH CONTINUED to immerse herself in her faith journey, she began to feel a sense of purpose she hadn't felt in a long time. She joined a small group at the church, where members shared their experiences and supported each other in their spiritual growth. The group became a source of strength and encouragement for Sarah.

One evening, during a small group meeting, Sarah shared her story with the group. She spoke about her struggles with faith after Michael's death and how the comforting presence had guided her back to the church. As she spoke, she noticed several group members nodding in understanding.

"Thank you for sharing, Sarah," said James, an older gentleman with kind eyes. "Your story is a powerful reminder that we're never truly alone, even in our darkest moments."

Another group member, Lisa, shared her own experience of losing a loved one and finding comfort in her faith. The stories resonated deeply with Sarah, reinforcing the idea that faith could provide solace and strength in times of grief.

The First Step Towards Healing

SARAH'S JOURNEY OF healing was not without its challenges. There were days when the pain of losing Michael felt unbearable, and her doubts resurfaced. But each time she felt overwhelmed, she turned to her faith and the comforting presence that had become a constant in her life.

One day, while volunteering at a church event, Sarah met a woman named Linda who had recently lost her husband. Linda was struggling with her grief and feeling lost, much like Sarah had been. Sarah listened to Linda's story with empathy and shared her own journey of finding faith and comfort.

"Sometimes, it feels like the pain will never go away," Linda said, tears streaming down her face. "How do you keep going?"

Sarah took Linda's hand and looked into her eyes. "It's not easy, and there are days when it feels impossible. But I've learned to lean on my faith and trust that there's a greater plan, even if I don't understand it. And the comforting presence I feel reminds me that I'm not alone."

Linda nodded, a glimmer of hope in her eyes. "Thank you, Sarah. It helps to know that someone else understands."

As they continued to talk, Sarah felt a sense of fulfillment. Helping Linda gave her a renewed sense of purpose and reinforced her belief in the power of faith and community.

Embracing the Future

AS MONTHS PASSED, SARAH'S faith grew stronger, and she found herself increasingly involved in church activities. She joined the worship team, using her love of music to connect with others and express her gratitude. She also became a mentor to new members, sharing her story and offering support to those struggling with their faith.

One Sunday, after a particularly uplifting service, Grace approached Sarah with a smile. "I've been thinking, Sarah. Would you be interested in leading a small group?"

Sarah was taken aback. "Me? Lead a group? I'm not sure I'm ready for that."

Grace placed a reassuring hand on her shoulder. "You've come so far, Sarah. Your journey is an inspiration to many, and I believe you have a lot to offer. Just think about it."

Over the next few days, Sarah prayed for guidance and sought the comforting presence that had become her silent companion. She felt a sense of peace and encouragement, as if the whispers were telling her to take this new step.

Finally, Sarah agreed to lead the group. It was a challenge, but it also brought immense joy and fulfillment. She found herself connecting with others on a deeper level, offering support and guidance, and witnessing their own journeys of faith and healing.

The Power of Faith and Community

AS THE YEARS WENT BY, Sarah's life continued to be shaped by her faith and the community she had built around her. She became a respected leader in the church, known for her compassion, wisdom, and unwavering faith.

The comforting presence remained with her, a constant reminder of the angels that had guided her through her darkest times. Sarah often reflected on her journey and the incredible transformation she had experienced.

One evening, as she sat in her favorite spot by the window, watching the sunset, she felt a deep sense of gratitude. She knew that her journey was far from over, but she was ready to face whatever challenges lay ahead with faith, hope, and the comforting presence of her angels.

Sarah bowed her head in prayer, her heart filled with peace. "Thank you, God, for guiding me back to faith and for the angels who have been with me every step of the way. I trust in Your plan and am grateful for the community and purpose You have given me."

As she finished her prayer, she felt the familiar warmth of the comforting presence, wrapping around her like a gentle embrace. Sarah smiled, knowing that she was never truly alone and that her journey of faith would continue to unfold in beautiful and unexpected ways.

Chapter 2: Signs and Wonders

Subtle Signs in Daily Life

Sarah's journey back to faith had begun, but it was only the start of a path lined with signs and wonders that would further solidify her beliefs. It started with small, seemingly inconsequential occurrences, which she initially dismissed as mere coincidences. But as these events became more frequent and undeniable, Sarah began to see the hand of the divine in her everyday life.

One crisp autumn morning, Sarah was on her way to work. The air was cool and the leaves crunched under her feet, painting a picturesque scene with shades of orange, yellow, and red. As she walked, she spotted a small white feather gently drifting down from the sky, landing directly in her path. She picked it up, smiling at the delicate beauty of it, but didn't think much of it at the time.

Later that day, as she was working at her desk, Sarah noticed a peculiar warmth surrounding her. It was as if someone had turned up the heat in her small office, yet the thermostat remained unchanged. The warmth seemed to radiate from within, giving her a sense of comfort and peace. She closed her eyes and took a deep breath, feeling an inexplicable calm wash over her.

That evening, Sarah was preparing dinner when she suddenly remembered a dream she'd had the night before. In the dream, she had been walking through a beautiful garden filled with flowers of every color. As she walked, a gentle voice had spoken to her, telling her to "trust in the signs." At the time, she had dismissed it as just a dream, but now, in the context of the day's events, it felt like more than that.

Sarah began to pay closer attention to her surroundings, looking for patterns and signs that might offer guidance. She noticed that whenever she felt particularly stressed or overwhelmed, the comforting warmth would return, calming her nerves and helping her focus. She started to see white feathers more frequently, often in the most unexpected places—on her doorstep, on the seat of her car, and even on the shelf of a bookstore she visited.

Regular Church Attendance

ENCOURAGED BY THESE experiences, Sarah started attending church more regularly. Each service left her feeling uplifted and hopeful, and she began to build a routine around her spiritual practices. She joined a Bible study group, where she met other members of the congregation and deepened her understanding of the scriptures. Her newfound community provided her with support and companionship, helping her feel less alone in her journey.

One Sunday, after a particularly moving sermon, Sarah decided to stay behind and speak with Pastor John. He was a kind and approachable man with a wealth of knowledge and a deep, abiding faith. Sarah had found his sermons to be both inspiring and thought-provoking, often addressing questions she had been grappling with herself.

As the last of the congregation filtered out of the sanctuary, Sarah approached Pastor John, who was tidying up the altar. "Pastor John, do you have a moment?" she asked hesitantly.

"Of course, Sarah," he replied with a warm smile. "What's on your mind?"

"I've been experiencing some... unusual things lately," Sarah began, trying to find the right words. "I keep seeing white feathers, feeling this strange warmth, and even hearing a voice in my dreams. It's comforting, but I'm not sure what to make of it."

Pastor John listened attentively, nodding as she spoke. "It sounds like you might be experiencing signs from the divine," he said thoughtfully. "Angels often communicate with us in subtle ways, using symbols and sensations that we can recognize. White feathers, in particular, are commonly associated with angels."

Sarah's eyes widened in surprise. "Really? I thought I was just imagining things."

"Not at all," Pastor John assured her. "God and His angels often reach out to us in ways that can seem small or coincidental, but they carry deep meaning. It's important to stay open to these signs and trust that you're being guided."

Meeting Pastor John

ENCOURAGED BY PASTOR John's words, Sarah felt a renewed sense of purpose. She continued to attend church regularly and became more involved in various activities and events. She joined a prayer group, helped with charity drives, and even started volunteering at the church's soup kitchen. The more she immersed herself in her faith community, the more she felt the comforting presence of the divine in her life.

One evening, after a particularly uplifting prayer meeting, Sarah stayed behind to help clean up. Pastor John was there, and they struck up a conversation about faith and divine intervention.

"Pastor John, have you ever experienced anything like what I've been describing?" Sarah asked, curious to hear his perspective.

Pastor John smiled knowingly. "I have, many times. In fact, my journey to becoming a pastor was filled with signs and wonders that I couldn't ignore. It's what led me to dedicate my life to serving God."

He went on to share stories of his own experiences, from miraculous healings to moments of profound insight that had guided his path. Sarah listened intently, feeling a deep connection to his stories and finding comfort in knowing she wasn't alone in her experiences.

Divine Interventions

AS THE WEEKS WENT BY, Sarah continued to notice subtle signs and wonders in her daily life. One afternoon, she was walking through a park when she saw a butterfly land on a nearby bench. Its wings were a brilliant shade of blue, shimmering in the sunlight. As she watched, the butterfly seemed to linger longer than usual, almost as if it were trying to convey a message. She took it as a sign of transformation and renewal, a reminder that she was on the right path.

Another time, while reading her Bible, she came across a passage that seemed to speak directly to her situation. It was from Isaiah 41:10: "Do not fear, for I am with you; do not be dismayed, for I am your God. I will strengthen you and help you; I will uphold you with my righteous right hand." The words resonated deeply with her, and she felt a sense of peace and reassurance.

One particularly memorable experience occurred during a visit to a friend's house. Sarah had been feeling particularly anxious that day, her mind racing with worries about her future. As she sat in her friend's living room, she noticed a beautiful painting on the wall depicting an angel with outstretched wings, surrounded by a soft, golden light. The painting seemed to radiate a calming energy, and Sarah felt her anxiety melt away.

That night, as she lay in bed, Sarah heard the soothing voice again, whispering words of encouragement and hope. "You are not alone," the voice said. "Trust in the signs, and know that you are loved and protected."

Moments of Doubt

DESPITE THESE COMFORTING experiences, Sarah still had moments of doubt. There were times when she questioned whether the signs she was seeing were real or simply products of her imagination. She struggled with feelings of inadequacy and fear, wondering if she was truly deserving of divine guidance.

During these times, the soothing voice would often make its presence known, offering words of encouragement and reassurance. "Have faith," the voice would whisper. "You are on the right path. Trust in the journey."

One evening, after a particularly challenging day, Sarah found herself feeling overwhelmed by doubt and uncertainty. She decided to take a walk to clear her mind and found herself at the church. The doors were open, and she stepped inside, seeking solace in the quiet sanctuary.

As she knelt in prayer, she felt the familiar warmth envelop her, and the soothing voice spoke softly in her heart. "You are loved, Sarah. Trust in the signs and wonders that surround you. They are gifts from the divine, guiding you on your path."

Tears filled Sarah's eyes as she felt the weight of her doubts lift. She knew that the journey of faith was not without its challenges, but she also knew that she was not alone. The signs and wonders she had experienced were tangible reminders of the divine presence in her life, offering guidance and support.

A Growing Faith

AS SARAH CONTINUED to navigate her faith journey, she found herself growing stronger and more confident in her beliefs. The signs and wonders she encountered became a source of inspiration and motivation, encouraging her to trust in the divine plan for her life.

One day, while volunteering at the church's soup kitchen, Sarah met a young woman named Emily who was struggling with her own faith. Emily had recently lost her job and was feeling lost and hopeless. Sarah listened to her story with compassion and shared her own experiences of finding faith and comfort in the midst of hardship.

"Sometimes, it feels like the world is against us," Sarah said gently. "But I've learned that there are signs and wonders all around us, reminding us that we are not alone. It's important to stay open to these messages and trust that we are being guided."

Emily nodded, tears in her eyes. "Thank you, Sarah. I've been so focused on my problems that I've forgotten to look for the signs. I'll try to keep my heart open."

As Sarah continued to support and encourage Emily, she felt a deep sense of fulfillment. Helping others find their faith and recognize the signs of divine intervention had become a central part of her own journey, and she was grateful for the opportunity to make a difference.

The Power of Community

THROUGHOUT HER JOURNEY, Sarah found that her faith was strengthened by the community she had become a part of. The members of her church were a constant source of support and encouragement, helping her navigate the challenges and uncertainties of life.

One Sunday, after a particularly moving service, the congregation gathered for a potluck lunch in the church hall. As Sarah mingled with friends old and new, she felt a deep sense of belonging and connection. The sense of community and shared faith was a powerful reminder that she was not alone on her journey.

During the meal, Pastor John stood up to address the congregation. "I'd like to share a story with you all," he began. "It's a story about signs and wonders, and how the divine often works in mysterious ways to guide and protect us."

He went on to recount a personal experience of divine intervention, describing how a series of seemingly unrelated events had led him to a crucial turning point in his life. The story resonated deeply with Sarah, and she felt a renewed sense of faith and trust in the divine plan.

As the afternoon drew to a close, Sarah found herself reflecting on the many signs and wonders she had encountered in her own life. From the comforting warmth and white feathers to the soothing voice and moments of profound insight, each experience had been a gift, guiding her on her journey of faith.

Embracing the Signs

AS SARAH CONTINUED to embrace the signs and wonders that surrounded her, she found herself growing more attuned to the subtle messages of the divine. She learned to trust her intuition and follow the guidance she received, knowing that she was being led by a higher power.

One evening, as she was journaling about her experiences, Sarah felt a sudden urge to visit a local park. It was a place she hadn't been to in years, but the feeling was so strong that she decided to follow it. She arrived at the park just as the sun was setting, casting a golden glow over the landscape.

As she walked along the winding paths, she felt a sense of peace and contentment. The air was filled with the sweet scent of blooming flowers, and the sound of birdsong provided a soothing backdrop. As she rounded a bend, she came across a small pond, its surface reflecting the colors of the sunset.

There, on the edge of the pond, was a bench with a plaque that read, "In Memory of Michael Langston." Sarah's breath caught in her throat as she realized that this was a place Michael had loved, a place he had often visited to find solace and inspiration.

Tears filled her eyes as she sat down on the bench, feeling a deep connection to Michael and the divine presence that had guided her to this moment. She closed her eyes and took a deep breath, feeling the comforting warmth envelop her once again.

The soothing voice spoke softly in her heart, offering words of encouragement and love. "Michael is with you, Sarah. He watches over you with love and pride. Trust in the signs and wonders that surround you, and know that you are never alone."

A New Beginning

AS SARAH SAT BY THE pond, reflecting on her journey, she felt a profound sense of gratitude. The signs and wonders she had experienced had not only guided her back to faith but had also helped her heal and find a new sense of purpose.

She decided to honor Michael's memory by dedicating herself to helping others find their own faith and recognize the signs of divine intervention in their lives. She knew that her journey was far from over, but she was ready to face whatever challenges lay ahead with faith, hope, and the comforting presence of her angels.

In the weeks that followed, Sarah began to share her story more openly, both within her church community and beyond. She started a blog where she wrote about her experiences, offering encouragement and support to others who were struggling with their faith. Her words resonated with many, and she received messages from people all over the world who had found comfort and inspiration in her story.

One day, Sarah received an invitation to speak at a local conference on faith and spirituality. Nervous but excited, she accepted the invitation and began preparing her speech. On the day of the conference, she stood before a packed audience, her heart pounding with anticipation.

"Hello, everyone," she began, her voice steady and confident. "My name is Sarah Langston, and I'd like to share with you my journey of faith and the signs and wonders that have guided me along the way."

As she spoke, she felt the comforting presence of her angels, offering her encouragement and strength. She shared her experiences of finding faith after Michael's death, the signs and wonders that had appeared in her daily life, and the profound impact they had on her journey.

The audience listened intently, moved by her story and inspired by her unwavering faith. When she finished, the room erupted in applause, and Sarah felt a deep sense of fulfillment and gratitude.

Continuing the Journey

SARAH'S JOURNEY OF faith continued to unfold in beautiful and unexpected ways. She remained open to the signs and wonders that surrounded her, trusting in the divine guidance that had become a central part of her life.

One evening, as she was reading her Bible, she came across a passage that spoke directly to her heart: "For I know the plans I have for you," declares the Lord, "plans to prosper you and not to harm you, plans to give you hope and a future" (Jeremiah 29:11). The words resonated deeply with her, reaffirming her belief in the divine plan for her life.

Sarah continued to dedicate herself to helping others find their faith and recognize the signs of divine intervention in their own lives. She became a sought-after speaker, sharing her story at conferences, churches, and community events. Her blog gained a large following, and she received countless messages from people who had been touched by her words.

Through it all, the comforting presence of her angels remained with her, offering guidance and encouragement. Sarah knew that her journey was far from over, but she was ready to face whatever challenges lay ahead with faith, hope, and the unwavering belief in the signs and wonders that had guided her every step of the way.

As she looked to the future, Sarah felt a profound sense of peace and contentment. She knew that she was never truly alone and that the divine presence in her life would continue to guide and protect her. With a heart full of gratitude and a spirit filled with faith, Sarah embraced the journey ahead, trusting in the signs and wonders that had become her constant companions.

Chapter 3: The Guardian's Presence

Discovering Guardian Angels

As Sarah delved deeper into her faith journey, she became increasingly curious about the concept of guardian angels. The comforting presence she had been experiencing led her to wonder if there were specific angels assigned to protect and guide her. During a Sunday service, Pastor John mentioned guardian angels in his sermon, sparking Sarah's interest even further.

After the service, she approached Pastor John with a question that had been on her mind. "Pastor John, can you tell me more about guardian angels? Do we all have one?"

Pastor John smiled warmly. "Yes, Sarah, many people believe that each of us is assigned a guardian angel by God. These angels watch over us, guide us, and protect us from harm. They often communicate through subtle signs and feelings, offering comfort and direction."

Sarah's curiosity grew. "How can I know if my guardian angel is around? Are there specific signs I should look for?"

"Everyone's experience is different," Pastor John explained. "Some people feel a sense of warmth or peace, while others might see specific symbols like feathers or hear a whisper in their hearts. The important thing is to stay open to these experiences and trust that your guardian angel is always with you, even if you can't see them."

Sarah nodded, feeling a deep sense of reassurance. "Thank you, Pastor John. I think I've felt my guardian angel's presence, but I wasn't sure if it was real."

"Trust in your experiences, Sarah," Pastor John encouraged. "Your guardian angel is there to help you on your journey of faith. Keep your heart open and listen to the whispers of guidance."

Feeling the Protective Presence

WITH THIS NEWFOUND understanding, Sarah began to pay even closer attention to the subtle signs and feelings she experienced. She often felt a warm, protective presence, especially during moments of doubt or fear. It was as if her guardian angel was wrapping her in a comforting embrace, assuring her that everything would be okay.

One evening, Sarah decided to take a walk through a nearby park to clear her mind. The sun was setting, casting a golden glow over the landscape, and the air was filled with the sweet scent of blooming flowers. As she walked, she felt the familiar warmth envelop her, bringing a sense of peace and tranquility.

As she rounded a bend, she noticed a small, secluded path leading into a wooded area. Curiosity piqued, she decided to explore it. The path was narrow and winding, lined with tall trees that formed a canopy overhead. The further she walked, the more isolated she felt from the rest of the park.

Suddenly, she heard a rustling sound in the bushes ahead. Her heart quickened, and she felt a surge of fear. But just as quickly, she felt the protective presence of her guardian angel, whispering words of reassurance. "Stay calm, Sarah. You are safe."

Taking a deep breath, she continued down the path, feeling the comforting warmth grow stronger. As she emerged from the wooded area, she saw a group of people up ahead, enjoying a picnic by the lake. Relief washed over her, and she realized that her guardian angel had guided her through the moment of fear.

Narrow Escape from Danger

A FEW DAYS LATER, SARAH experienced a situation that would further reinforce her belief in the protective presence of her guardian angel. She was driving home from work on a rainy evening, the roads slick with water and visibility poor. As she navigated a particularly sharp curve, she suddenly lost control of her car. The vehicle skidded across the road, heading straight for a ditch.

Panic surged through her, but just as quickly, she heard the soothing whisper of her guardian angel. "Stay calm. Turn the wheel gently." Following the guidance, she managed to regain control of the car and steer it back onto the road. Her heart pounded in her chest as she pulled over to the side, shaken but unharmed.

As she sat in her car, catching her breath, Sarah realized how close she had come to a serious accident. She knew without a doubt that her guardian angel had protected her, guiding her through the dangerous situation and keeping her safe.

That night, as she lay in bed, Sarah felt the comforting warmth of her guardian angel envelop her once again. She whispered a prayer of gratitude, thanking God for the divine protection and guidance she had received. "Thank you for keeping me safe," she prayed. "I trust in your presence and guidance."

Keeping a Journal

INSPIRED BY HER EXPERIENCES, Sarah decided to start keeping a journal to document the signs and wonders she encountered, as well as the guidance and protection she felt from her guardian angel. She hoped that writing about these experiences would help her better understand and appreciate the divine presence in her life.

Her first journal entry described the incident on the road, detailing how she had felt her guardian angel's guidance and protection. She wrote about the fear she had experienced and the soothing whisper that had helped her regain control of her car. As she wrote, she felt a deep sense of gratitude and awe for the divine presence that had saved her.

Over the next few weeks, Sarah continued to document her experiences in her journal. She wrote about the subtle signs she noticed, the moments of comfort and peace she felt, and the whispers of guidance she received. Each entry reinforced her belief in the presence of her guardian angel and helped her feel more connected to her faith.

One evening, as she was writing in her journal, Sarah felt a sudden urge to reflect on the journey she had been on since Michael's death. She wrote about her struggles with faith, the comforting presence she had felt, and the signs and wonders that had guided her back to the church. As she poured her heart onto the pages, she realized how far she had come and how much she had grown.

Sharing Her Experiences

AS SARAH CONTINUED to document her experiences, she felt a growing desire to share her story with others. She hoped that by sharing her journey, she could offer encouragement and support to those who were struggling with their own faith.

One Sunday, after a particularly moving service, Sarah approached Pastor John with an idea. "Pastor John, I've been keeping a journal of my experiences with my guardian angel and the signs and wonders I've encountered. I was thinking that maybe I could share my story with the congregation."

Pastor John smiled warmly. "That's a wonderful idea, Sarah. Your story is a powerful testament to the presence of God and His angels in our lives. I'm sure it will inspire and uplift many people."

With Pastor John's encouragement, Sarah prepared to share her story during the next Sunday service. She was nervous, but she knew that her experiences could offer hope and encouragement to others who were struggling with their faith.

On the day of the service, Sarah stood before the congregation, her heart pounding with anticipation. She took a deep breath and began to speak. "Hello, everyone. My name is Sarah Langston, and I'd like to share with you my journey of faith and the experiences I've had with my guardian angel."

As she spoke, she felt the comforting presence of her guardian angel, offering her encouragement and strength. She shared her story of finding faith after Michael's death, the signs and wonders that had appeared in her daily life, and the profound impact they had on her journey.

The congregation listened intently, moved by her story and inspired by her unwavering faith. When she finished, the room erupted in applause, and Sarah felt a deep sense of fulfillment and gratitude.

Continuing the Journey

SARAH'S JOURNEY OF faith continued to unfold in beautiful and unexpected ways. She remained open to the signs and wonders that surrounded her, trusting in the divine guidance that had become a central part of her life.

One evening, as she was reading her Bible, she came across a passage that spoke directly to her heart: "For He will command His angels concerning you to guard you in all your ways" (Psalm 91:11). The words resonated deeply with her, reaffirming her belief in the presence of her guardian angel.

Sarah continued to dedicate herself to helping others find their faith and recognize the signs of divine intervention in their own lives. She became a sought-after speaker, sharing her story at conferences, churches, and community events. Her blog gained a large following, and she received countless messages from people who had been touched by her words.

Through it all, the comforting presence of her guardian angel remained with her, offering guidance and encouragement. Sarah knew that her journey was far from over, but she was ready to face whatever challenges lay ahead with faith, hope, and the unwavering belief in the presence of her guardian angel.

A New Challenge

ONE MORNING, AS SARAH was going through her daily routine, she received an unexpected phone call from her friend Grace. "Sarah, I need your help," Grace said, her voice filled with urgency. "There's a family in our community who's in desperate need of support. They've been through a lot, and I think you could really make a difference."

Sarah didn't hesitate. "Of course, Grace. Tell me more about the situation."

Grace explained that the family had recently lost their home in a fire and were struggling to get back on their feet. They had been staying in a temporary shelter, but they needed more support to rebuild their lives. Grace was organizing a community effort to help them, and she believed that Sarah's story and experiences could offer them hope and encouragement.

Sarah felt a deep sense of compassion for the family and knew that this was an opportunity to put her faith into action. She agreed to meet with the family and offer whatever support she could.

Offering Hope and Encouragement

WHEN SARAH MET THE family, she was struck by their resilience and strength in the face of adversity. They shared their story of loss and struggle, and Sarah listened with empathy and understanding. She could see the pain and uncertainty in their eyes, and she knew that they needed more than just material support—they needed hope and encouragement.

Drawing from her own experiences, Sarah shared her journey of faith and the signs and wonders that had guided her through difficult times. She spoke about the presence of her guardian angel and how it had offered her comfort and protection. As she spoke, she saw a glimmer of hope in their eyes, and she knew that her words were making a difference.

"Thank you, Sarah," the mother of the family said, tears in her eyes. "Your story gives us hope. It reminds us that we are not alone and that there is a higher power watching over us."

Sarah felt a deep sense of fulfillment and gratitude. She knew that her guardian angel had guided her to this moment, giving her the opportunity to make a difference in the lives of others. She continued to offer support to the family, helping them find resources and connecting them with the community.

Documenting the Experience

THAT EVENING, SARAH sat down with her journal to document the experience. She wrote about the family's resilience and strength, the hope she saw in their eyes, and the sense of fulfillment she felt in offering them support. As she wrote, she felt the comforting presence of her guardian angel, reassuring her that she was on the right path.

She also reflected on the journey she had been on since Michael's death. She had come so far, growing in her faith and finding a sense of purpose in helping others. The signs and wonders she had experienced had guided her every step of the way, offering comfort and protection.

Sarah realized that her journey was far from over, and she felt a deep sense of excitement for what lay ahead. She knew that her guardian angel would continue to guide and protect her, helping her navigate the challenges and uncertainties of life.

Embracing the Future

AS SARAH CONTINUED her journey, she remained open to the signs and wonders that surrounded her, trusting in the divine guidance that had become a central part of her life. She knew that her guardian angel was always with her, offering comfort and protection in moments of doubt and fear.

One evening, as she was journaling about her experiences, she felt a sudden urge to visit a nearby lake. It was a place she hadn't been to in years, but the feeling was so strong that she decided to follow it. She arrived at the lake just as the sun was setting, casting a golden glow over the water.

As she walked along the shore, she felt the familiar warmth envelop her, bringing a sense of peace and tranquility. She sat down on a bench overlooking the lake, taking in the beauty of the moment.

The soothing voice of her guardian angel spoke softly in her heart, offering words of encouragement and love. "You are not alone, Sarah. Trust in the signs and wonders that surround you. They are gifts from the divine, guiding you on your path."

Tears filled Sarah's eyes as she felt the weight of her doubts lift. She knew that the journey of faith was not without its challenges, but she also knew that she was not alone. The signs and wonders she had experienced were tangible reminders of the divine presence in her life, offering guidance and support.

As she looked to the future, Sarah felt a profound sense of peace and contentment. She knew that she was never truly alone and that the divine presence in her life would continue to guide and protect her. With a heart full of gratitude and a spirit filled with faith, Sarah embraced the journey ahead, trusting in the signs and wonders that had become her constant companions.

Chapter 4: A Test of Faith

Facing a Significant Challenge

Sarah's journey of faith had been filled with signs and wonders, providing her with comfort and guidance during difficult times. However, she knew that her faith would eventually be tested in more significant ways. This test came in the form of a major challenge at work that threatened to unravel the progress she had made.

Sarah worked as a project manager at a mid-sized marketing firm. The job was demanding but rewarding, and she had built a reputation for being reliable and efficient. However, the company had recently taken on a high-profile client, and the pressure to deliver exceptional results was immense. The project was complex, involving multiple teams and tight deadlines, and Sarah was appointed as the lead manager.

From the outset, the project was fraught with difficulties. Key team members fell ill, software glitches caused delays, and communication breakdowns led to misunderstandings and mistakes. Sarah found herself working late into the night, trying to keep everything on track. Despite her best efforts, it seemed like the project was spiraling out of control.

The stress began to take its toll on Sarah, and she found herself questioning her ability to handle the situation. Her newfound faith, which had been a source of strength, now felt distant and inaccessible. Doubt crept into her mind, and she began to wonder if she was truly capable of leading the project to success.

Praying for Guidance

ONE PARTICULARLY STRESSFUL evening, after a long day of setbacks, Sarah sat alone in her office, feeling overwhelmed and defeated. She had tried everything she could think of to get the project back on track, but nothing seemed to be working. Desperation drove her to her knees, and she bowed her head in prayer.

"Dear God," she whispered, her voice trembling. "I don't know what to do. I've tried so hard, but everything is falling apart. Please, show me the way. Give me the strength and wisdom to handle this challenge. I need your guidance."

As she prayed, Sarah felt the familiar warmth of her guardian angel envelop her. It was a comforting reminder that she was not alone, even in her darkest moments. She took a deep breath, feeling a sense of peace wash over her. She knew that she needed to trust in the divine guidance that had brought her this far.

Unexpected Help

THE NEXT MORNING, SARAH arrived at work with a renewed sense of determination. She was greeted by a kind colleague named Emily, who had always been friendly and supportive. Emily noticed the strain on Sarah's face and approached her with concern.

"Sarah, you look exhausted. Is everything okay?" Emily asked gently.

Sarah sighed, feeling the weight of the world on her shoulders. "It's this project. It's been a nightmare, and I don't know how to fix it. I've tried everything, but nothing seems to be working."

Emily's eyes softened with understanding. "I'm sorry you're going through this. If there's anything I can do to help, please let me know."

Sarah hesitated for a moment, unsure of how to respond. She had always been independent and self-reliant, but she realized that she needed help. "Actually, there is something you could do. I could use another set of eyes on the project plan. Maybe you'll see something I've missed."

"Of course, I'd be happy to help," Emily replied with a reassuring smile. "Let's sit down and go over it together."

As they reviewed the project plan, Emily offered valuable insights and suggestions that Sarah hadn't considered. Her fresh perspective helped identify areas where improvements could be made, and together, they developed a new strategy to tackle the issues.

Sarah was amazed at how much progress they made in just a few hours. She couldn't help but feel that Emily's timely assistance was more than just a coincidence. It felt like a direct answer to her prayer, and she believed that her guardian angel had guided Emily to help her.

Whispers of Encouragement

OVER THE NEXT FEW DAYS, Sarah noticed that the whispers of her guardian angel grew more frequent. They offered words of encouragement and guidance, helping her navigate the challenges she faced. Whenever she felt overwhelmed or uncertain, the soothing voice would remind her to stay calm and trust in the divine plan.

One afternoon, as Sarah was dealing with a particularly difficult client request, she felt the familiar warmth of her guardian angel. The whisper came softly, urging her to approach the situation with patience and understanding. Taking a deep breath, she followed the guidance and managed to resolve the issue without further conflict.

The more she listened to the whispers, the more confident she became in her ability to handle the project. She began to see each challenge as an opportunity to grow in her faith and trust in the divine guidance that had been with her all along.

Overcoming the Obstacles

WITH EMILY'S HELP AND the guidance of her guardian angel, Sarah began to turn the project around. The team rallied together, inspired by her renewed sense of determination and faith. They worked tirelessly to meet the deadlines, and gradually, the setbacks began to diminish.

Sarah's leadership shone through as she navigated the team through the complexities of the project. She implemented the changes that Emily had suggested and encouraged open communication among the team members. Her ability to stay calm under pressure and her unwavering belief in their success motivated everyone to give their best effort.

One evening, as Sarah was reviewing the progress they had made, she felt a deep sense of gratitude. She knew that she couldn't have done it alone.

The support from Emily, the guidance of her guardian angel, and her own determination had all played a crucial role in overcoming the obstacles.

A Moment of Reflection

AS THE PROJECT NEARED completion, Sarah took a moment to reflect on the journey she had been on. She thought about the challenges she had faced and the moments of doubt that had tested her faith. Through it all, she had found strength in her prayers and the comforting presence of her guardian angel.

Sarah realized that her faith had grown stronger through the experience. She had learned to trust in the divine plan, even when things seemed impossible. The whispers of guidance and the unexpected help from Emily had shown her that she was never truly alone.

One evening, after a long day of work, Sarah sat down with her journal to document her experiences. She wrote about the challenges she had faced, the prayers she had offered, and the divine guidance that had helped her overcome the obstacles. As she wrote, she felt a deep sense of peace and fulfillment.

Sharing Her Story

INSPIRED BY HER EXPERIENCES, Sarah decided to share her story with the congregation once again. She hoped that her journey of faith and the challenges she had overcome would offer encouragement and inspiration to others.

On the day of the service, Sarah stood before the congregation, her heart filled with gratitude and humility. "Hello, everyone," she began. "I'd like to share with you a recent experience that tested my faith and showed me the power of divine guidance."

As she spoke, she felt the comforting presence of her guardian angel, offering her encouragement and strength. She shared the story of the project at work, the moments of doubt and desperation, and the unexpected help she had received from Emily. She spoke about the whispers of guidance and the sense of peace that had carried her through the difficult times.

The congregation listened intently, moved by her story and inspired by her unwavering faith. When she finished, the room erupted in applause, and Sarah felt a deep sense of fulfillment and gratitude.

Continuing the Journey

SARAH'S JOURNEY OF faith continued to unfold, guided by the signs and wonders that had become a central part of her life. She knew that there would be more challenges ahead, but she was ready to face them with faith, hope, and the unwavering belief in the presence of her guardian angel.

One evening, as she was reading her Bible, she came across a passage that spoke directly to her heart: "Trust in the Lord with all your heart and lean not on your own understanding; in all your ways submit to Him, and He will make your paths straight" (Proverbs 3:5-6). The words resonated deeply with her, reaffirming her belief in the divine plan for her life.

Sarah continued to dedicate herself to helping others find their faith and recognize the signs of divine intervention in their own lives. She became a sought-after speaker, sharing her story at conferences, churches, and community events. Her blog gained a large following, and she received countless messages from people who had been touched by her words.

Through it all, the comforting presence of her guardian angel remained with her, offering guidance and encouragement. Sarah knew that her journey was far from over, but she was ready to face whatever challenges lay ahead with faith, hope, and the unwavering belief in the presence of her guardian angel.

The Importance of Community

SARAH'S FAITH JOURNEY was enriched by the sense of community she had found at her church. The support and encouragement from Pastor John, Emily, and the other members of the congregation played a crucial role in helping her navigate the challenges she faced.

One Sunday, after the service, Sarah joined a small group discussion led by Pastor John. The topic was "Faith in Times of Adversity," and it resonated deeply with her. As the group shared their experiences, Sarah felt a sense of camaraderie and understanding. She realized that everyone faced challenges and doubts, but their shared faith and support for one another helped them overcome these obstacles.

Sarah decided to open up about her recent experience at work. She shared how the project had tested her faith and how the guidance of her guardian angel and the unexpected help from Emily had been instrumental in overcoming the challenges. The group listened attentively, and several members shared their own stories of divine intervention and support from their guardian angels.

Pastor John concluded the discussion with a powerful message. "Faith is not about having all the answers or never facing difficulties. It's about trusting in God's plan, even when we don't understand it. It's about being open to the signs and wonders that guide us and leaning on our community for support. Together, we can face any challenge with faith and hope."

Sarah felt a deep sense of gratitude for the community that had become such an important part of her life. Their support and shared experiences had strengthened her faith and helped her navigate the challenges she faced.

A New Sense of Purpose

AS SARAH CONTINUED her journey of faith, she found herself drawn to new opportunities to help others. She realized that her experiences had given her a unique perspective and the ability to offer support and encouragement to those who were struggling.

One day, while volunteering at a local shelter, Sarah met a young woman named Lisa who was going through a difficult time. Lisa had recently lost her job and was feeling hopeless and alone. Sarah listened to her story with empathy and shared her own journey of faith and the challenges she had overcome.

"Sometimes, it feels like everything is falling apart," Sarah said gently. "But I've learned that even in our darkest moments, there are signs and wonders guiding us. It's important to stay open to these messages and trust that we are being led to a better place."

Lisa's eyes filled with tears. "Thank you, Sarah. Your words give me hope. I've been so focused on my problems that I haven't been able to see the signs. I'll try to keep my heart open."

Sarah felt a deep sense of fulfillment as she offered support and encouragement to Lisa. She realized that her journey of faith had given her a new sense of purpose—to help others find their own faith and recognize the signs of divine intervention in their lives.

Embracing the Future

AS SARAH CONTINUED to navigate her journey of faith, she remained open to the signs and wonders that surrounded her. She trusted in the guidance of her guardian angel and the divine plan for her life. She knew that there would be more challenges ahead, but she was ready to face them with faith, hope, and the unwavering belief in the presence of her guardian angel.

One evening, as she was journaling about her experiences, she felt a sudden urge to visit a nearby park. It was a place she hadn't been to in years, but the feeling was so strong that she decided to follow it. She arrived at the park just as the sun was setting, casting a golden glow over the landscape.

As she walked along the winding paths, she felt a sense of peace and contentment. The air was filled with the sweet scent of blooming flowers, and the sound of birdsong provided a soothing backdrop. As she rounded a bend, she came across a small pond, its surface reflecting the colors of the sunset.

There, on the edge of the pond, was a bench with a plaque that read, "In Memory of Michael Langston." Sarah's breath caught in her throat as she realized that this was a place Michael had loved, a place he had often visited to find solace and inspiration.

Tears filled her eyes as she sat down on the bench, feeling a deep connection to Michael and the divine presence that had guided her to this moment. She closed her eyes and took a deep breath, feeling the comforting warmth envelop her once again.

The soothing voice of her guardian angel spoke softly in her heart, offering words of encouragement and love. "Michael is with you, Sarah. He watches over you with love and pride. Trust in the signs and wonders that surround you, and know that you are never alone."

As she looked to the future, Sarah felt a profound sense of peace and contentment. She knew that she was never truly alone and that the divine presence in her life would continue to guide and protect her. With a heart full of gratitude and a spirit filled with faith, Sarah embraced the journey ahead, trusting in the signs and wonders that had become her constant companions.

Conclusion

Sarah's journey of faith had been marked by challenges, doubts, and moments of despair. But through it all, she had found strength in her prayers, the guidance of her guardian angel, and the support of her community. The signs and wonders she had encountered had reaffirmed her belief in the divine plan for her life and helped her navigate the uncertainties and obstacles she faced.

As she continued her journey, Sarah remained open to the signs and wonders that surrounded her, trusting in the guidance of her guardian angel and the divine plan for her life. She knew that there would be more challenges ahead, but she was ready to face them with faith, hope, and the unwavering belief in the presence of her guardian angel.

With a heart full of gratitude and a spirit filled with faith, Sarah embraced the journey ahead, knowing that she was never truly alone. The signs and wonders that had guided her every step of the way would continue to be her constant companions, offering comfort, guidance, and hope as she navigated the path of faith.

In her journal, Sarah wrote a final entry for the chapter, summarizing her thoughts and reflections: "Faith is not about having all the answers or never facing difficulties. It's about trusting in God's plan, even when we don't understand it. It's about being open to the signs and wonders that guide us and leaning on our community for support. Together, we can face any challenge with faith and hope."

As she closed her journal, Sarah felt a deep sense of peace and contentment. She knew that her journey of faith was far from over, but she was ready to face whatever lay ahead with faith, hope, and the unwavering belief in the presence of her guardian angel.

Chapter 5: The Healing Touch

A Friend in Need

Sarah's life had taken on a serene rhythm, woven with threads of faith and guided by the whispers of her guardian angel. She had come to trust in the divine signs and wonders that had consistently led her through challenges. However, a new trial was about to test her faith in a way she had never experienced before.

One crisp autumn afternoon, Sarah received an unexpected phone call from Grace's husband, David. His voice was strained and filled with worry. "Sarah, it's Grace. She's very sick. We're at the hospital, and things aren't looking good."

Sarah's heart sank. Grace was more than a friend; she was a beacon of strength and faith, the person who had helped guide Sarah back to church and supported her through her darkest times. Hearing that she was seriously ill felt like a punch to the gut. "I'm coming right away," Sarah said, her voice trembling.

She rushed to the hospital, her mind racing with worry and prayers. Upon arrival, she found David in the waiting room, looking pale and exhausted. He explained that Grace had been diagnosed with a severe infection that had quickly escalated, leading to complications. The doctors were doing everything they could, but the situation was critical.

Sarah hugged David tightly, offering him whatever comfort she could muster. "We have to believe that she'll pull through," she said, more to convince herself than him. "Grace is strong, and she has so many people praying for her."

Fervent Prayers

SARAH SPENT THE NEXT several days at the hospital, keeping vigil by Grace's bedside and praying fervently for her recovery. She witnessed the relentless efforts of the medical staff and the constant beeping of machines that monitored Grace's fragile condition. It was a stark reminder of how fragile life could be.

One evening, as Sarah sat in the hospital chapel, she bowed her head in earnest prayer. "Dear God, please heal Grace. She's been a source of strength and faith for so many, including me. We need her. Please, send your healing touch to restore her health."

As she prayed, Sarah felt the comforting warmth of her guardian angel envelop her, offering reassurance and hope. She clung to her faith, believing that divine intervention could make a difference. The whispers of her guardian angel became more frequent, offering words of encouragement and urging her to trust in the healing power of prayer.

Witnessing the Angelic Figure

ONE NIGHT, AS SARAH kept vigil in Grace's hospital room, she found herself dozing off in the chair beside the bed. The room was dimly lit, the only sounds being the soft hum of medical equipment and the rhythmic beep of the heart monitor.

Sarah woke suddenly, feeling a presence in the room. As she opened her eyes, she saw a faint, glowing light near Grace's bed. At first, she thought she was dreaming or that her eyes were playing tricks on her, but the light grew brighter, forming the shape of a figure. It was ethereal and radiant, with an aura of pure, comforting light.

The figure stood by Grace's bedside, reaching out a hand to gently touch her forehead. Sarah's breath caught in her throat as she watched, feeling a profound sense of peace and awe. The figure's presence was overwhelmingly soothing, and Sarah instinctively knew that she was witnessing something divine.

The figure turned its head slightly, as if acknowledging Sarah's presence, and then slowly faded away, leaving the room in darkness once more. Sarah blinked, unsure of what she had just seen, but the sense of peace remained. She felt tears streaming down her face as she whispered a prayer of gratitude. "Thank you, God, for sending your angel. Please, let this be a sign that Grace will recover."

The Miracle of Recovery

THE NEXT MORNING, SARAH was awoken by the sound of hushed voices and hurried footsteps. She quickly realized that something had changed. The medical staff was bustling around Grace's bed, but their expressions were no longer filled with worry. There was a sense of hope and excitement in the air.

A nurse approached Sarah with a smile. "Grace's condition has improved significantly overnight. Her fever has broken, and her vital signs are stabilizing. It's nothing short of a miracle."

Sarah felt a wave of relief and gratitude wash over her. She knew in her heart that the angelic figure she had witnessed had played a role in Grace's recovery. She rushed to Grace's bedside, where David was already holding her hand, tears of joy in his eyes.

Grace's eyes fluttered open, and she smiled weakly. "Sarah, David... I feel better," she whispered.

David kissed her hand, his voice choked with emotion. "You've been so strong, Grace. We've been praying for you, and it looks like those prayers have been answered."

Sarah couldn't hold back her tears. "I saw an angel, Grace. Last night, in this room. I believe it was here to heal you."

Grace's eyes filled with wonder. "An angel? Oh, Sarah... I felt something. I felt a warmth and peace, even in my feverish state. I believe it too."

Strengthening Faith

GRACE'S RECOVERY CONTINUED over the following days, her strength gradually returning. The doctors were amazed at her rapid improvement, and many referred to it as a miraculous turnaround. For Sarah, witnessing Grace's recovery and the angelic figure had profoundly strengthened her belief in angels and divine intervention.

One afternoon, as Sarah and Grace sat together in the hospital room, Sarah shared more details about the angelic figure she had seen. "It was so beautiful,

Grace. Radiant and peaceful, like nothing I've ever seen before. I knew it was there to help you."

Grace nodded, her eyes shining with gratitude. "I believe it too, Sarah. I've always had faith, but this experience has taken it to a whole new level. I feel so blessed to have had you by my side, praying for me."

Sarah smiled, squeezing Grace's hand. "We're both blessed, Grace. This experience has strengthened my faith more than I could have imagined. I feel like I've been given a glimpse of the divine, and it's something I'll never forget."

Sharing the Miracle

AS GRACE CONTINUED to recover, Sarah felt a growing desire to share the story of the angelic visitation and the miraculous healing with others. She believed that their experience could offer hope and inspiration to those who were struggling with their faith.

One Sunday, Sarah and Grace stood before the congregation, ready to share their story. The church was filled with familiar faces, all eager to hear about Grace's recovery. Pastor John introduced them, his voice filled with warmth and admiration.

"Today, we have a powerful testimony to share," he began. "Sarah and Grace have experienced a miracle, and their story is a testament to the power of prayer and the presence of angels in our lives."

Sarah took a deep breath and began to speak. "Hello, everyone. I want to share with you the incredible journey that Grace and I have been on over the past few weeks. Grace fell seriously ill, and the doctors were unsure if she would make it. But through fervent prayer and divine intervention, we witnessed a miracle."

She went on to describe the angelic figure she had seen in Grace's hospital room, the sense of peace it had brought, and the miraculous recovery that followed. Grace then shared her own perspective, speaking about the warmth and comfort she had felt during her illness and her unwavering belief in the power of faith.

The congregation listened intently, moved by their story. When they finished, the room erupted in applause, and many people approached them afterward to offer their support and share their own experiences of faith and healing.

Documenting the Miracle

INSPIRED BY THE RESPONSE from the congregation, Sarah decided to document the miracle in her journal. She wanted to capture every detail, from the moment she received the call about Grace's illness to the angelic visitation and Grace's miraculous recovery.

As she wrote, Sarah felt a deep sense of gratitude and awe. She realized how far she had come on her journey of faith and how each experience had strengthened her belief in the divine. The signs and wonders she had encountered, the guidance of her guardian angel, and now the miraculous healing had all been part of a greater plan.

Sarah's journal entry read: "Today, I witnessed a miracle. Grace's recovery is a testament to the power of prayer and the presence of angels in our lives. I saw an angel, radiant and peaceful, bringing healing and comfort to my dear friend. This experience has strengthened my faith in ways I could never have imagined. I am grateful for the divine guidance and protection that has been with me every step of the way."

Moving Forward

AS GRACE CONTINUED to regain her strength, Sarah felt a renewed sense of purpose. She knew that her journey of faith was far from over, and she was eager to see where it would lead her next. The experience of witnessing an angelic figure and the miraculous healing had deepened her belief in the divine and reinforced her commitment to helping others find their faith.

One evening, as Sarah and Grace sat together in the garden, Grace spoke about her plans for the future. "I've been thinking a lot about what I want to do when I'm fully recovered," she said. "I feel like I've been given a second chance, and I want to use it to make a difference."

Sarah nodded, understanding the sentiment. "I've been feeling the same way. This experience has shown me how powerful faith can be, and I want to help others find that same sense of peace and comfort."

Grace smiled, her eyes filled with determination. "I was thinking about starting a support group for people who are going through difficult times. A place where they can share their stories, find comfort in prayer, and lean on each other for support. What do you think?"

Sarah's heart swelled with pride and admiration for her friend. "I think that's a wonderful idea, Grace. And I'd love to help in any way I can."

The Support Group

OVER THE NEXT FEW WEEKS, Sarah and Grace worked together to establish the support group. They spread the word through the church and the community, inviting anyone who was seeking comfort and support to join. The response was overwhelmingly positive, and soon, they had a small but dedicated group of people who were eager to share their experiences and find solace in their faith.

The first meeting was held in the church's community room, and Sarah felt a mix of excitement and nervousness as she prepared to welcome the participants. Grace stood beside her, offering a reassuring smile. "We're doing something good here, Sarah. I can feel it."

As the group members arrived, Sarah and Grace greeted each one with warmth and kindness. They began the meeting with a prayer, asking for divine guidance and support for everyone in the room. Then, they invited each participant to share their story, creating a safe and supportive space for everyone to open up.

The stories that were shared were filled with pain and struggle, but also with hope and resilience. Sarah was deeply moved by the courage and strength of each person, and she felt a profound sense of gratitude for the opportunity to be a part of their journey.

As the meeting came to a close, Sarah and Grace offered words of encouragement and support to the group. They reminded everyone that they were not alone and that their faith could provide comfort and guidance through even the darkest times.

A New Chapter

THE SUPPORT GROUP QUICKLY became an important part of Sarah and Grace's lives. Each meeting was filled with powerful stories, heartfelt prayers, and a sense of community that strengthened everyone's faith. Sarah felt a deep sense of fulfillment and purpose, knowing that she was making a difference in the lives of others.

One evening, after a particularly moving meeting, Sarah sat down with her journal to reflect on the journey she had been on. She wrote about the challenges she had faced, the signs and wonders she had encountered, and the miraculous healing that had strengthened her faith.

Her journal entry read: "Today, I am filled with gratitude for the journey I have been on. From the darkest moments of doubt to the miraculous healing that strengthened my faith, I have seen the hand of the divine in every step. The support group that Grace and I have started is a testament to the power of faith and community. I am grateful for the opportunity to help others find their own faith and comfort in the presence of angels."

As she closed her journal, Sarah felt a deep sense of peace and contentment. She knew that her journey of faith was far from over, but she was ready to face whatever challenges lay ahead with faith, hope, and the unwavering belief in the presence of her guardian angel.

Embracing the Future

SARAH'S JOURNEY OF faith had taken her through trials and triumphs, each experience strengthening her belief in the divine. The miraculous healing of Grace had been a pivotal moment, reinforcing her trust in the power of prayer and the presence of angels. As she looked to the future, Sarah felt a sense of excitement and anticipation for what lay ahead.

One day, as she and Grace were preparing for another support group meeting, Sarah received a phone call from Pastor John. "Sarah, I have an opportunity I'd like to discuss with you," he said. "There's a conference on faith and healing coming up, and I think you and Grace would be wonderful speakers. Your story is incredibly inspiring, and I believe it could offer hope to many."

Sarah was both surprised and honored by the invitation. She had never considered herself a public speaker, but the thought of sharing their story on a larger platform was both exciting and daunting. "Thank you, Pastor John. I'm honored. I'll discuss it with Grace, and we'll get back to you."

Grace was equally surprised but enthusiastic about the idea. "Sarah, this is a wonderful opportunity to share our journey and inspire others. I think we should do it."

After discussing the details and praying for guidance, Sarah and Grace decided to accept the invitation. They spent the next few weeks preparing their presentation, reflecting on their experiences and the lessons they had learned. They wanted to convey the power of faith, the presence of angels, and the importance of community in a way that would resonate with the audience.

The Conference

THE DAY OF THE CONFERENCE arrived, and Sarah and Grace found themselves standing before a large audience, ready to share their story. The room was filled with people from all walks of life, each one seeking inspiration and hope.

Pastor John introduced them with a heartfelt speech, highlighting their journey and the impact they had made in their community. As Sarah and Grace took the stage, Sarah felt a familiar sense of warmth and comfort, knowing that her guardian angel was with her.

"Hello, everyone," Sarah began, her voice steady and confident. "My name is Sarah, and this is my dear friend Grace. We're here to share our journey of faith and the miraculous healing that has strengthened our belief in the presence of angels."

They spoke about the challenges they had faced, the prayers they had offered, and the angelic visitation that had brought healing and comfort. They shared the story of the support group and the powerful sense of community that had emerged from their efforts. The audience listened intently, many moved to tears by their heartfelt testimony.

When they finished, the room erupted in applause, and Sarah felt a deep sense of fulfillment and gratitude. Many people approached them afterward, expressing their admiration and sharing their own experiences of faith and healing. Sarah and Grace spent the rest of the day connecting with the attendees, offering words of encouragement and support.

Continuing the Journey

THE CONFERENCE WAS a turning point for Sarah and Grace, opening new doors and opportunities to share their story and inspire others. They received invitations to speak at other events, and their support group grew in size and impact. Sarah felt a profound sense of purpose, knowing that she was making a difference in the lives of others.

One evening, as Sarah sat in her favorite spot by the window, watching the sunset, she reflected on the incredible journey she had been on. From the darkest moments of doubt to the miraculous healing that had strengthened her faith, she had seen the hand of the divine in every step. The signs and wonders she had encountered, the guidance of her guardian angel, and the support of her community had all been part of a greater plan.

Sarah opened her journal and wrote a final entry for the chapter: "Today, I am filled with gratitude for the journey I have been on. The miraculous healing of Grace has reinforced my belief in the power of prayer and the presence of angels. Our support group and the opportunity to share our story at the conference have shown me the importance of faith and community. I am ready to embrace the future with faith, hope, and the unwavering belief in the presence of my guardian angel."

As she closed her journal, Sarah felt a deep sense of peace and contentment. She knew that her journey of faith was far from over, but she was ready to face whatever challenges lay ahead with faith, hope, and the unwavering belief in the presence of her guardian angel.

With a heart full of gratitude and a spirit filled with faith, Sarah embraced the journey ahead, trusting in the signs and wonders that had become her constant companions. She knew that she was never truly alone and that the divine presence in her life would continue to guide and protect her. The healing touch of her guardian angel had brought her this far, and she was ready to continue her journey, knowing that the best was yet to come.

Chapter 6: Angelic Encounters

Researching Angels

Sarah's journey of faith had been profoundly shaped by the divine encounters and miraculous experiences she had witnessed. The healing of Grace, guided by the angelic figure she had seen, strengthened her belief in angels and their presence in our lives. Driven by curiosity and a desire to understand more about these celestial beings, Sarah began to immerse herself in researching angels.

She visited the local library and spent hours poring over books on angelology, the study of angels. She read ancient texts, theological treatises, and modern accounts of angelic encounters. Each book provided a different perspective, but common themes emerged: angels as messengers of God, protectors, and guides for those in need.

One book, in particular, captivated her. It was titled "Angelic Visitations: A Collection of True Stories," edited by a theologian named Dr. Margaret O'Connor. The book compiled personal testimonies from people around the world who had experienced angelic encounters. The stories ranged from miraculous healings and life-saving interventions to comforting presences during times of grief.

Sarah found herself deeply moved by the accounts. She felt a connection to the people who shared their experiences, recognizing the same sense of awe and gratitude she had felt when she saw the angel in Grace's hospital room. These stories reinforced her belief in the presence of angels and the divine plan guiding her life.

Joining the Church Group

AS SARAH DELVED DEEPER into her research, she discovered that her church had a special group dedicated to angelic encounters. The group, called "Heavenly Hosts," met once a month to share experiences, study angelology, and support one another in their spiritual journeys. Excited by the prospect of connecting with others who shared her interest, Sarah decided to join the group.

The next meeting of Heavenly Hosts was held in a cozy room at the church. Sarah entered the room with a mix of anticipation and nervousness. She was greeted by a warm and welcoming atmosphere, with soft lighting and comfortable chairs arranged in a circle. A table in the center held a collection of angel figurines, candles, and a Bible.

The group's leader, a kind woman named Linda, introduced herself and invited Sarah to join the circle. Linda explained that the group was a safe space for sharing personal experiences, exploring the role of angels in their lives, and seeking guidance through prayer and meditation.

"We're here to support each other and grow in our faith," Linda said with a smile. "Everyone's experience is unique, and we believe that sharing our stories can bring us closer to understanding the divine presence of angels."

Sharing Her Story

AS THE MEETING BEGAN, Linda invited each member to introduce themselves and share their most recent angelic encounter. Sarah listened intently as the members recounted their stories, each one filled with awe and wonder. Some spoke of dreams where angels had delivered messages, while others described moments of protection and guidance during difficult times.

When it was Sarah's turn, she took a deep breath and began to share her story. "My name is Sarah, and I'm relatively new to this group. I wanted to join because I've had some profound experiences with angels, and I wanted to connect with others who have had similar encounters."

She recounted the story of Grace's illness, the fervent prayers, and the miraculous recovery guided by the angelic figure she had witnessed in the hospital room. As she spoke, she felt a deep sense of connection with the group, knowing that they understood and believed in the presence of angels just as she did.

The group listened with rapt attention, their faces reflecting a mix of admiration and empathy. When Sarah finished, Linda reached out and gently squeezed her hand. "Thank you for sharing your story, Sarah. It's truly inspiring and a testament to the power of faith and the presence of angels."

Hearing Other Stories

AS THE MEETING CONTINUED, other members shared their stories, each one adding to the tapestry of angelic encounters that filled the room. Sarah found herself deeply moved by the diversity of experiences and the common thread of divine guidance and protection.

One woman, named Alice, shared a story of a car accident she had been in a few years ago. "I was driving home on a rainy night when I lost control of my car," Alice began. "I remember feeling terrified as my car skidded off the road and headed toward a ditch. But then, out of nowhere, I felt a strong presence in the car with me. It was as if someone took the wheel and guided me back onto the road. I managed to stop the car safely, and when I looked around, there was no one else in the car. I believe it was my guardian angel."

Another member, Tom, spoke about a time when he had been struggling with severe depression. "I felt completely lost and alone," Tom said, his voice trembling with emotion. "One night, I was contemplating ending my life when I suddenly felt a warm, comforting presence. I heard a voice whispering, 'You are loved. Don't give up.' That moment changed everything for me. I believe it was an angel sent to save me."

Each story resonated deeply with Sarah, reinforcing her belief in the presence of angels and the importance of sharing these experiences. She felt a profound sense of validation and community, knowing that she was not alone in her encounters with the divine.

The Power of Community

AS THE WEEKS WENT BY, Sarah continued to attend the Heavenly Hosts meetings, finding solace and strength in the shared experiences of the group.

The meetings became a cornerstone of her spiritual journey, providing a space for reflection, learning, and mutual support.

One evening, Linda announced that the group would be hosting a special event: a guest speaker who had written extensively about angelic encounters. The speaker, Dr. Margaret O'Connor, was the same theologian whose book Sarah had found so inspiring. Excited by the opportunity to meet her, Sarah eagerly anticipated the event.

The night of the event arrived, and the church was filled with people eager to hear Dr. O'Connor speak. Sarah found a seat near the front, her heart racing with anticipation. As Dr. O'Connor took the stage, she exuded a sense of calm and wisdom that immediately put the audience at ease.

"Good evening, everyone," Dr. O'Connor began. "Thank you for inviting me to speak with you tonight. I've spent many years studying angels and collecting stories of angelic encounters from people all over the world. Each story is a testament to the divine presence in our lives and the ways in which angels guide and protect us."

She shared several stories from her book, each one more awe-inspiring than the last. She spoke about the different types of angels, their roles as messengers and protectors, and the ways in which they communicate with us. Dr. O'Connor emphasized the importance of staying open to these encounters and trusting in the divine guidance they offer.

After her talk, Dr. O'Connor invited the audience to ask questions and share their own experiences. Sarah hesitated for a moment before raising her hand. "Dr. O'Connor, your book has been incredibly inspiring to me. I've had my own encounters with angels, and they've strengthened my faith in ways I never thought possible. How can we continue to cultivate this connection and remain open to angelic guidance?"

Dr. O'Connor smiled warmly. "Thank you for sharing, Sarah. Cultivating a connection with angels involves staying open to the signs and messages they send, practicing prayer and meditation, and surrounding yourself with a supportive community, like this group. Trust in your experiences and know that angels are always with you, guiding and protecting you."

Deepening the Connection

INSPIRED BY DR. O'CONNOR'S words, Sarah felt a renewed sense of purpose in her spiritual journey. She continued to attend the Heavenly Hosts meetings, deepening her connection with the group and finding new ways to cultivate her relationship with angels.

One evening, Linda introduced a new activity for the group: guided meditations focused on connecting with angels. The idea was to create a space for quiet reflection and open the mind and heart to the presence of angels. Sarah was intrigued and eager to participate.

The group gathered in a circle, and Linda led them through the meditation. "Close your eyes and take a deep breath," she began. "Imagine yourself surrounded by a warm, comforting light. This light is the presence of your guardian angel, here to guide and protect you. Feel their love and warmth enveloping you."

As Sarah followed Linda's guidance, she felt the familiar warmth of her guardian angel. She visualized the angelic figure she had seen in Grace's hospital room, radiating peace and love. In her mind's eye, she saw the angel reaching out to touch her hand, offering comfort and reassurance.

"Now, ask your angel for guidance," Linda continued. "Listen for any messages or insights they may have for you. Trust in their presence and know that you are never alone."

In the quiet of the meditation, Sarah felt a deep sense of connection with her guardian angel. She heard the soothing whispers of encouragement and felt a renewed sense of peace and purpose. The experience was profoundly moving, and she felt a surge of gratitude for the divine presence in her life.

The Healing Power of Stories

AS THE GROUP CONTINUED to share their stories and experiences, Sarah noticed the profound impact these stories had on each member. The act of sharing and listening created a sense of solidarity and understanding, reinforcing their belief in the divine and strengthening their faith.

One evening, a new member named Rachel joined the group. She was hesitant and unsure, having recently experienced a traumatic event that had shaken her faith. Linda welcomed her warmly and invited her to share her story if she felt comfortable.

Rachel took a deep breath and began to speak. "A few months ago, I was in a terrible car accident. I survived, but I lost my fiancé. The grief has been overwhelming, and I've struggled to find any sense of peace. I've always believed in angels, but lately, I've felt so disconnected from my faith."

The group listened with empathy and understanding, offering words of comfort and support. Sarah felt a deep connection to Rachel's story, remembering her own struggles with grief after losing Michael.

After Rachel finished, Sarah spoke up. "Rachel, thank you for sharing your story. I know how difficult it can be to find faith after such a profound loss. I've been through something similar, and I found solace in the presence of angels and the support of this community. You're not alone, and we're here to help you find your way."

Rachel nodded, tears in her eyes. "Thank you, Sarah. It means a lot to know that others understand and that there's hope for healing."

A Community of Faith

THE HEAVENLY HOSTS group continued to grow, attracting new members and deepening their connection with one another. The meetings became a place of refuge and inspiration, where each member felt valued and supported in their spiritual journey.

Sarah found herself becoming more involved in the group's activities, helping Linda organize events and leading guided meditations. She felt a deep sense of fulfillment in her role, knowing that she was making a difference in the lives of others.

One evening, as the group gathered for their monthly meeting, Linda announced a special project: a book compiling the stories of their angelic encounters. "I believe that our experiences have the power to inspire and uplift others," Linda said. "By sharing our stories, we can spread the message of faith and the presence of angels to a wider audience."

The group was enthusiastic about the idea, and each member agreed to contribute their story. Sarah felt a surge of excitement at the prospect of sharing their collective experiences with the world.

Writing the Book

THE PROCESS OF WRITING the book was a labor of love for the Heavenly Hosts group. Each member took the time to carefully document their encounters, reflecting on the impact these experiences had on their lives. The stories were filled with awe, gratitude, and a deep sense of connection to the divine.

Sarah's contribution focused on the healing of Grace and the angelic figure she had witnessed in the hospital room. She wrote about the prayers, the fervent hope, and the miraculous recovery that had strengthened her faith. She also included her experiences with the support group and the profound sense of community and validation she had found.

As the stories came together, the group felt a deep sense of pride and accomplishment. They had created something beautiful and meaningful, a testament to the power of faith and the presence of angels in their lives.

Sharing the Message

THE BOOK, TITLED "ANGELIC Encounters: True Stories of Faith and Healing," was published and quickly gained attention. The Heavenly Hosts group held a special event at the church to celebrate its release, inviting the community to come and hear the stories that had inspired them.

Sarah felt a mix of excitement and nervousness as she prepared to speak at the event. She stood before the audience, her heart filled with gratitude for the journey she had been on and the people who had supported her along the way.

"Hello, everyone," Sarah began. "We're here today to celebrate the release of our book, 'Angelic Encounters.' This book is a collection of true stories from our group, each one a testament to the presence of angels and the power of faith. We've poured our hearts into these stories, and we hope they will inspire and uplift you as they have us."

She went on to share her own story, speaking about the healing of Grace and the angelic figure she had seen. She spoke about the support group and the sense of community and validation they had found in one another. The audience listened intently, moved by her words and the collective experiences of the group.

When the event concluded, many people approached Sarah and the other members, expressing their admiration and gratitude. The book had touched their hearts, offering hope and inspiration in their own spiritual journeys.

A Continuing Journey

AS SARAH REFLECTED on the journey that had led her to this point, she felt a profound sense of fulfillment and purpose. The angelic encounters, the support group, and the book had all been part of a greater plan, guiding her to a deeper understanding of faith and the presence of angels.

She knew that her journey was far from over and that there would be more challenges and opportunities ahead. But she felt ready to face them, strengthened by the knowledge that she was never alone. The signs and wonders she had experienced, the guidance of her guardian angel, and the support of her community had all been part of a greater plan.

One evening, as Sarah sat in her favorite spot by the window, she opened her journal and wrote a final entry for the chapter: "Today, I am filled with gratitude for the journey I have been on. The angelic encounters, the support group, and the book have all been part of a greater plan, guiding me to a deeper understanding of faith and the presence of angels. I am ready to embrace the future with faith, hope, and the unwavering belief in the presence of my guardian angel."

As she closed her journal, Sarah felt a deep sense of peace and contentment. She knew that her journey of faith was far from over, but she was ready to face whatever challenges lay ahead with faith, hope, and the unwavering belief in the presence of her guardian angel.

With a heart full of gratitude and a spirit filled with faith, Sarah embraced the journey ahead, trusting in the signs and wonders that had become her constant companions. She knew that she was never truly alone and that the divine presence in her life would continue to guide and protect her. The angelic encounters had brought her this far, and she was ready to continue her journey, knowing that the best was yet to come.

Chapter 7: A New Mission

A Calling to Serve

Sarah's journey of faith had taken her through profound experiences, each encounter with angels deepening her belief in the divine. The miraculous healing of Grace, the angelic encounters she shared with the Heavenly Hosts group, and the impact of their book, "Angelic Encounters: True Stories of Faith and Healing," had all fortified her faith and purpose. She felt an undeniable calling to help others who were struggling with their faith, to offer them the same hope and guidance she had received.

One evening, after a particularly moving Heavenly Hosts meeting, Sarah found herself reflecting on her journey. She felt a strong urge to expand her efforts beyond the group and the church, to reach out to those who were in desperate need of hope and comfort. She prayed for guidance, asking God to show her how she could best serve others.

As she sat in quiet meditation, she felt the familiar warmth of her guardian angel envelop her. The soothing whispers came, offering reassurance and direction. "Seek those in need, offer your heart and hands. Your journey of faith has prepared you to help others find theirs."

Inspired by the message, Sarah decided to volunteer at a local shelter. She had heard about the shelter from a friend and knew it provided support for individuals and families facing homelessness, addiction, and other crises. It seemed like the perfect place to start her new mission.

Volunteering at the Shelter

SARAH CONTACTED THE shelter and arranged to meet with the volunteer coordinator, a kind woman named Maria. The shelter was located in a modest building in a less affluent part of town, but it was a beacon of hope for many who sought refuge there.

When Sarah arrived, she was greeted by Maria, who gave her a tour of the facility. The shelter was bustling with activity, volunteers and staff working tirelessly to provide meals, clothing, and support services to those in need. Sarah was struck by the sense of community and compassion that permeated the space.

"We're always grateful for new volunteers," Maria said with a warm smile. "There are so many ways you can help, whether it's serving meals, organizing donations, or providing emotional support to our guests. What draws you to this kind of work, if you don't mind me asking?"

Sarah shared her story with Maria, explaining her journey of faith and the angelic encounters that had inspired her to help others. Maria listened intently, her eyes reflecting understanding and empathy. "Your story is truly inspiring, Sarah. I believe you'll be a great asset to our team and a source of hope for our guests."

Meeting Incredible People

SARAH BEGAN VOLUNTEERING at the shelter several times a week, dedicating her time to serving meals, sorting donations, and offering a listening ear to those who sought her out. She quickly realized that the shelter was a place of incredible stories, many of which involved moments of divine intervention and angelic encounters.

One afternoon, while serving lunch, Sarah met an elderly man named James. He had a gentle demeanor and a twinkle in his eye that hinted at a life filled with remarkable experiences. As they chatted over a meal, James began to share his story.

"I haven't always been homeless," James said, his voice tinged with nostalgia. "I used to have a good job and a family, but things fell apart. I lost everything—my job, my home, and eventually my faith. I was wandering the streets, feeling completely lost, when something extraordinary happened."

James described a night when he was sleeping under a bridge, feeling cold and hopeless. "I was at my lowest point, ready to give up, when I felt a warm presence beside me. I opened my eyes and saw a figure bathed in light, sitting next to me. It didn't speak, but I felt an overwhelming sense of peace and love. The figure stayed with me until morning, and when I woke up, I found a bag of food and a blanket beside me. I knew then that I wasn't alone and that someone was watching over me."

Sarah was deeply moved by James's story. "That sounds like a divine encounter, James. Angels often appear to us in our times of greatest need, offering comfort and guidance."

James nodded, tears glistening in his eyes. "That experience restored my faith, Sarah. I've faced many challenges since then, but I hold on to the memory of that night. It's what keeps me going."

The Whispers of Guidance

AS SARAH CONTINUED to volunteer at the shelter, she found that the whispers of her guardian angel grew more frequent and clear. They offered guidance and encouragement, helping her navigate the complexities of her new mission. The whispers often came at the most unexpected times, offering insights that seemed almost miraculous.

One evening, as Sarah was organizing donations, she noticed a young woman sitting alone in the corner of the room. The woman looked distressed, her eyes red from crying. Sarah felt a gentle nudge from her guardian angel, urging her to approach the woman.

"Hi there," Sarah said softly, sitting down next to her. "I'm Sarah. Is there anything I can do to help?"

The woman looked up, her expression a mix of fear and desperation. "I'm Lisa," she replied. "I don't know where to start. I've been living on the streets for weeks, and I feel like I've lost everything."

Sarah listened as Lisa shared her story. She had recently fled an abusive relationship and had nowhere else to go. She felt isolated and terrified, unsure of how to rebuild her life. Sarah's heart ached for her, and she knew that she needed to offer more than just words of comfort.

"Lisa, you're not alone," Sarah said gently. "There are people here who care about you and want to help. Let's take it one step at a time. We can start by finding you some clean clothes and a safe place to stay tonight."

With the guidance of the whispers, Sarah helped Lisa navigate the resources available at the shelter. They found her a bed for the night and connected her with a caseworker who could assist her with finding more permanent housing and support services. Sarah stayed by Lisa's side, offering a listening ear and a comforting presence.

Building Trust and Offering Hope

OVER THE NEXT FEW WEEKS, Sarah continued to support Lisa, helping her navigate the challenges of rebuilding her life. She became a source of stability and hope for Lisa, who began to open up and trust in the process.

One afternoon, as they sat together in the shelter's courtyard, Lisa shared a moment that had given her hope. "Last night, I had a dream," Lisa said, her voice filled with wonder. "I was standing in a field of flowers, and a figure bathed in light approached me. It didn't speak, but I felt an overwhelming sense of peace and love. When I woke up, I knew that I wasn't alone and that there was hope for me."

Sarah smiled, recognizing the divine nature of the dream. "It sounds like you had an angelic encounter, Lisa. Angels often appear to us in dreams, offering comfort and guidance. Hold on to that feeling of peace and know that you are being watched over."

Lisa nodded, tears of gratitude in her eyes. "Thank you, Sarah. You've been a beacon of hope for me. I don't know what I would have done without your support."

Sarah felt a deep sense of fulfillment, knowing that she was making a difference in Lisa's life. The whispers of her guardian angel continued to guide her, helping her offer the right words and actions at the right times.

Expanding Her Mission

AS SARAH'S WORK AT the shelter continued, she felt a growing desire to expand her mission and reach even more people in need. She began to explore ways to collaborate with other organizations and churches, creating a network of support for those struggling with their faith and facing difficult circumstances.

She reached out to Pastor John and shared her vision. "I believe we can do more to support our community," Sarah said. "There are so many people who need help and hope. By working together, we can create a stronger network of support and make a bigger impact."

Pastor John was supportive and enthusiastic about the idea. "I think it's a wonderful initiative, Sarah. Our church has always been committed to serving those in need, and this is a great way to expand our efforts. Let's organize a meeting with other community leaders and see how we can collaborate."

The meeting was held at the church, bringing together representatives from various organizations, including shelters, food banks, and counseling services. Sarah shared her vision and the impact of her work at the shelter, highlighting the importance of providing both practical support and spiritual guidance.

The response was overwhelmingly positive, and plans were set in motion to create a coordinated network of support. They decided to hold regular meetings to share resources, plan joint events, and offer training for volunteers on providing emotional and spiritual support.

Touching More Lives

WITH THE NEW NETWORK in place, Sarah's mission began to touch more lives. The collaboration allowed them to pool their resources and offer more comprehensive support to those in need. Sarah continued her work at the shelter but also began to take on a more active role in organizing and coordinating efforts across the network.

One day, while visiting a partnering food bank, Sarah met a woman named Maria who had recently lost her job and was struggling to provide for her children. Maria was overwhelmed and desperate, unsure of how to navigate the challenges she faced.

Sarah sat down with Maria, offering a listening ear and words of encouragement. "I know things seem impossible right now, but there is hope," Sarah said gently. "We have a network of support here, and we can help you find the resources you need to get back on your feet."

Maria was hesitant at first but slowly began to open up. With Sarah's guidance, they connected Maria with job placement services, childcare support, and counseling. Sarah also introduced Maria to the Heavenly Hosts group, where she found a supportive community that embraced her and offered spiritual guidance.

Maria's situation gradually improved, and she began to regain her confidence and hope. She found a new job and stable housing for her family, and her faith was strengthened by the support and love she received from the community.

The Whispers Continue

THROUGHOUT HER WORK, the whispers of Sarah's guardian angel remained a constant source of guidance and reassurance. They helped her navigate the complexities of her mission, offering insights and encouragement at every turn.

One evening, as Sarah was preparing for a support group meeting, she felt a strong nudge from her guardian angel. The whispers urged her to share a specific message of hope and resilience with the group.

"Tonight, I want to talk about the power of faith in overcoming adversity," Sarah began, addressing the group. "We've all faced challenges that seemed insurmountable, but it's our faith and the support of those around us that help us find the strength to keep going. I believe that each of us has the power to overcome our struggles and find hope in even the darkest times."

As she spoke, Sarah noticed the impact her words had on the group. Faces that had been filled with doubt and despair began to soften, and she saw tears of gratitude and understanding. The whispers guided her to share personal anecdotes and stories of angelic encounters, reinforcing the message of hope and resilience.

After the meeting, several group members approached Sarah, expressing their gratitude for her words. One woman, named Janet, shared how Sarah's message had resonated deeply with her. "I've been struggling with my faith for a long time," Janet said. "But your words tonight reminded me that I'm not alone and that there's always hope. Thank you for sharing that message."

Sarah felt a deep sense of fulfillment, knowing that she was making a difference in the lives of others. The whispers of her guardian angel continued to guide her, helping her offer the right words and actions at the right times.

Reflecting on the Journey

AS SARAH'S MISSION continued to expand, she took time to reflect on the incredible journey she had been on. From the initial encounters with angels that had strengthened her faith, to the profound impact of her work at the shelter and the support group, she felt a deep sense of gratitude for the divine guidance that had led her every step of the way.

One evening, as she sat in her favorite spot by the window, Sarah opened her journal and began to write: "Today, I am filled with gratitude for the journey I have been on. The angelic encounters, the support group, and the mission to help those in need have all been part of a greater plan, guiding me to a deeper understanding of faith and the presence of angels. I am ready to embrace the future with faith, hope, and the unwavering belief in the presence of my guardian angel."

As she closed her journal, Sarah felt a deep sense of peace and contentment. She knew that her journey of faith was far from over, but she was ready to face whatever challenges lay ahead with faith, hope, and the unwavering belief in the presence of her guardian angel.

Embracing the Future

SARAH'S MISSION TO help others continued to evolve, guided by the whispers of her guardian angel and the support of her community. She felt a profound sense of purpose and fulfillment in her work, knowing that she was making a difference in the lives of those who were struggling with their faith and facing difficult circumstances.

One day, while volunteering at the shelter, Sarah received a call from Maria, the shelter's volunteer coordinator. "Sarah, I wanted to let you know that we've been so impressed with your dedication and the impact you've made here. We'd like to offer you a more permanent role as our Community Outreach Coordinator. You'd be responsible for organizing events, coordinating with our network partners, and providing support to our guests. What do you think?"

Sarah was both surprised and honored by the offer. She felt a deep sense of gratitude for the opportunity to expand her mission and continue her work in a more official capacity. "Thank you, Maria. I would be honored to accept the role. I'm excited to continue making a difference and helping those in need."

With her new role, Sarah was able to take her mission to new heights. She organized community events that brought together volunteers, guests, and network partners, fostering a sense of unity and support. She also developed programs that focused on spiritual guidance and emotional healing, helping individuals find their faith and regain hope.

Stories of Hope

AS SARAH CONTINUED her work, she encountered countless stories of hope and resilience. Each story reinforced her belief in the power of faith and the presence of angels in our lives.

One evening, she met a man named Thomas who had recently lost his job and was struggling to provide for his family. Thomas was feeling overwhelmed and hopeless, unsure of how to move forward. Sarah sat down with him, offering a listening ear and words of encouragement.

"Thomas, I know things seem impossible right now, but there is always hope," Sarah said gently. "I've seen people overcome incredible challenges through faith and the support of their community. You are not alone, and we are here to help you."

Thomas shared his story, and Sarah helped him connect with job placement services, financial assistance programs, and counseling support. She also introduced him to the Heavenly Hosts group, where he found a supportive community that embraced him and offered spiritual guidance.

Over time, Thomas's situation began to improve. He found a new job, regained his confidence, and his faith was strengthened by the support and love he received from the community. He shared his gratitude with Sarah, expressing how her guidance and the presence of the support group had made a significant difference in his life.

Continuing the Mission

SARAH'S JOURNEY OF faith and service continued to evolve, guided by the whispers of her guardian angel and the support of her community. She felt a profound sense of purpose and fulfillment in her work, knowing that she was making a difference in the lives of those who were struggling with their faith and facing difficult circumstances.

One day, as she was preparing for a support group meeting, Sarah received a call from Pastor John. "Sarah, I've been hearing so many wonderful things about your work at the shelter and the impact of the support group. I wanted to invite you to speak at our upcoming community event. It's a gathering of faith leaders and community members, and I believe your story and mission would be incredibly inspiring."

Sarah was honored by the invitation and agreed to speak at the event. She spent the next few days preparing her presentation, reflecting on her journey and the lessons she had learned.

On the day of the event, Sarah stood before the audience, her heart filled with gratitude and humility. "Hello, everyone," she began. "My name is Sarah, and I'm here to share my journey of faith and the mission that has guided me to help those in need. I've had the incredible privilege of witnessing the power of faith and the presence of angels in our lives, and I believe that each of us has the ability to make a difference."

She spoke about her initial encounters with angels, the healing of Grace, and the impact of the Heavenly Hosts group. She shared stories from her work at the shelter, highlighting the resilience and hope she had seen in the people she had helped. Sarah emphasized the importance of community and the power of faith in overcoming adversity.

The audience listened intently, moved by her words and the collective experiences she shared. When she finished, the room erupted in applause, and many people approached her afterward to express their admiration and gratitude.

Embracing the Journey

AS SARAH REFLECTED on the journey that had led her to this point, she felt a profound sense of fulfillment and purpose. The angelic encounters, the support group, and her mission to help those in need had all been part of a greater plan, guiding her to a deeper understanding of faith and the presence of angels.

She knew that her journey was far from over and that there would be more challenges and opportunities ahead. But she felt ready to face them, strengthened by the knowledge that she was never alone. The signs and wonders she had experienced, the guidance of her guardian angel, and the support of her community had all been part of a greater plan.

One evening, as Sarah sat in her favorite spot by the window, she opened her journal and wrote a final entry for the chapter: "Today, I am filled with gratitude for the journey I have been on. The angelic encounters, the support group, and the mission to help those in need have all been part of a greater plan, guiding me to a deeper understanding of faith and the presence of angels. I am ready to embrace the future with faith, hope, and the unwavering belief in the presence of my guardian angel."

As she closed her journal, Sarah felt a deep sense of peace and contentment. She knew that her journey of faith was far from over, but she was ready to face whatever challenges lay ahead with faith, hope, and the unwavering belief in the presence of her guardian angel.

With a heart full of gratitude and a spirit filled with faith, Sarah embraced the journey ahead, trusting in the signs and wonders that had become her constant companions. She knew that she was never truly alone and that the divine presence in her life would continue to guide and protect her. The mission to help others had brought her this far, and she was ready to continue her journey, knowing that the best was yet to come.

Chapter 8: Doubts and Struggles

Moments of Doubt

Despite Sarah's remarkable journey of faith and her numerous angelic encounters, she found herself grappling with moments of doubt and spiritual struggle. These feelings often surfaced during quiet moments, when she was alone with her thoughts, reflecting on her experiences and the challenges she faced.

One evening, after a long day at the shelter, Sarah sat by her window, watching the sun set behind the distant hills. The sky was painted with hues of orange and pink, a sight that usually brought her peace. But tonight, a heaviness settled over her heart. She found herself questioning the purpose of her mission and whether she was truly making a difference in the lives of those she aimed to help.

Sarah thought about the people she had met at the shelter, the stories of hardship and pain they had shared. She remembered James, whose faith had been restored by an angelic encounter, and Lisa, who had fled an abusive relationship and was slowly rebuilding her life. Yet, despite these successes, there were many others who continued to struggle, their situations seemingly unchanged.

The doubts gnawed at her. Was she really helping, or was she merely offering temporary relief in an unending cycle of suffering? Was her faith enough to sustain her and those she aimed to support? The whispers that had once been a source of constant reassurance now felt distant, their presence overshadowed by her inner turmoil.

Confiding in Pastor John

IN SEARCH OF CLARITY and comfort, Sarah decided to confide in Pastor John. Over the years, he had been a steadfast mentor and friend, guiding her through her spiritual journey with wisdom and compassion. She trusted him to help her navigate this period of doubt.

On a quiet afternoon, Sarah visited Pastor John's office at the church. The familiar surroundings brought a sense of solace, even as her heart felt heavy with uncertainty. Pastor John greeted her warmly, his eyes reflecting genuine concern.

"Sarah, it's good to see you. Please, come in," he said, motioning to a comfortable chair across from his desk.

"Thank you, Pastor John," Sarah replied, taking a seat. "I needed to talk to you. I'm struggling with some doubts, and I don't know how to move past them."

Pastor John nodded, encouraging her to continue. "I'm here to listen, Sarah. What's been troubling you?"

Sarah took a deep breath, trying to articulate the thoughts that had been weighing on her mind. "I've had so many incredible experiences—angelic encounters, miracles, and the sense of divine guidance. But despite all of that, I still find myself doubting. I question whether my efforts are truly making a difference. Sometimes, it feels like I'm just putting a band-aid on a wound that won't heal."

Pastor John listened intently, his expression thoughtful. "It's natural to have doubts, Sarah. Faith isn't about having all the answers or never experiencing uncertainty. It's about trusting in God's plan, even when we can't see the full picture. Doubts are a part of the journey, and they can help us grow stronger in our faith."

Understanding the Importance of Faith

PASTOR JOHN LEANED forward, his voice gentle but firm. "Sarah, your work at the shelter and your mission to help others are not in vain. Each act of kindness, each moment of support, makes a difference, even if you can't always see the immediate results. The impact of your efforts may not always be visible, but that doesn't mean they aren't significant."

He paused, allowing his words to sink in before continuing. "Remember the story of the mustard seed? Jesus taught that faith, even as small as a mustard seed, can move mountains. Your faith and your actions, no matter how small they may seem, are powerful. They plant seeds of hope and change in the lives of those you touch."

Sarah felt a glimmer of hope at Pastor John's words. "But what about the times when I feel disconnected, when the whispers of guidance seem distant?"

"Those moments are a test of your faith," Pastor John explained. "It's easy to trust when we feel God's presence clearly. The real challenge is to maintain that trust even when we feel alone or uncertain. In those times, lean on your community, your support network, and the teachings of your faith. And remember, God is always with you, even if you can't feel it."

The Whispers of Reassurance

AFTER THEIR CONVERSATION, Sarah felt a renewed sense of purpose, but she knew that the journey of overcoming doubt was ongoing. She continued her work at the shelter, finding solace in the routine and the small victories that marked her days. The whispers of her guardian angel, though sometimes faint, began to reemerge, offering reassurance and guidance.

One evening, while helping a young mother named Rachel find resources for her family, Sarah felt the familiar warmth of her guardian angel. Rachel had recently escaped an abusive relationship and was struggling to provide for her children. Her story mirrored Lisa's in many ways, and Sarah felt a deep connection to her plight.

As Sarah listened to Rachel's fears and frustrations, the whispers offered words of encouragement. "You are making a difference, Sarah. Each act of kindness brings light into the darkness. Trust in your purpose."

Sarah shared her own journey with Rachel, offering hope and practical advice. "I know it's hard right now, but you're not alone. There are people here who care about you and want to help. Let's take it one step at a time."

Rachel's eyes filled with tears, and she nodded gratefully. "Thank you, Sarah. Your words mean a lot. I was starting to lose hope, but talking to you makes me believe that things can get better."

Finding Strength in Community

SARAH'S RENEWED SENSE of purpose was bolstered by the support of her community. The Heavenly Hosts group continued to be a source of strength and inspiration, as they shared their own experiences and supported each other through their spiritual journeys.

During one meeting, Linda, the group's leader, introduced a new member named Mark. He was a soft-spoken man in his late thirties, with an air of quiet determination. Mark shared his story, explaining that he had recently lost his job and was struggling to find direction in his life.

"I've always believed in angels and divine guidance," Mark said, his voice steady but tinged with uncertainty. "But lately, I've been feeling lost. It's hard to hold on to faith when everything seems to be falling apart."

The group listened with empathy, offering words of support and encouragement. Sarah felt a strong connection to Mark's story, recognizing her own struggles in his words. When it was her turn to speak, she shared her recent doubts and the conversation she had with Pastor John.

"Faith isn't about never having doubts," Sarah said. "It's about trusting in God's plan, even when we can't see the full picture. Each of us has moments of struggle, but it's our faith and our community that help us through."

Mark nodded, gratitude evident in his eyes. "Thank you, Sarah. It helps to know that I'm not alone in feeling this way."

Embracing the Journey

AS SARAH CONTINUED to navigate her doubts and struggles, she found solace in the knowledge that she was not alone. The whispers of her guardian angel, the support of her community, and the wisdom of Pastor John all reinforced her belief in the divine presence guiding her life.

One evening, as Sarah was journaling about her experiences, she felt a sudden urge to reflect on the journey she had been on. She thought about the miraculous healing of Grace, the angelic encounters, and the impact of her work at the shelter. Each experience had shaped her faith, strengthening her belief in the presence of angels and the power of divine guidance.

Her journal entry read: "Today, I am reminded that faith is a journey, filled with moments of doubt and uncertainty. But it is also a journey of trust and hope, guided by the whispers of angels and the support of my community. I am grateful for the lessons I've learned and the people who have walked this path with me. Together, we find strength in our faith and in each other."

As she closed her journal, Sarah felt a deep sense of peace and contentment. She knew that her journey of faith was far from over, but she was ready to face whatever challenges lay ahead with faith, hope, and the unwavering belief in the presence of her guardian angel.

Continuing the Mission

SARAH'S MISSION TO help others continued to evolve, guided by the whispers of her guardian angel and the support of her community. She felt a profound sense of purpose and fulfillment in her work, knowing that she was making a difference in the lives of those who were struggling with their faith and facing difficult circumstances.

One day, while volunteering at the shelter, Sarah met a young man named David who had recently lost his home and was struggling with addiction. David was withdrawn and reluctant to engage with anyone, his eyes reflecting a deep sense of hopelessness.

Sarah approached him gently, offering a warm smile. "Hi, David. I'm Sarah. Is there anything I can do to help?"

David looked up, his expression guarded. "I don't know if anyone can help me," he muttered. "I've made too many mistakes."

Sarah sat down beside him, her heart aching for his pain. "We all make mistakes, David. But that doesn't mean we can't find a way forward. There are people here who care about you and want to help. Let's take it one step at a time."

As they talked, Sarah felt the whispers of her guardian angel guiding her. She shared stories of others who had faced similar struggles and found hope and healing. Slowly, David began to open up, sharing his fears and frustrations.

Over the next few weeks, Sarah worked closely with David, helping him access the resources he needed to address his addiction and find stable housing. She introduced him to the Heavenly Hosts group, where he found a supportive community that embraced him and offered spiritual guidance.

Embracing the Future

AS SARAH CONTINUED her mission, she felt a deep sense of gratitude for the journey she had been on and the people who had supported her along the way. The doubts and struggles she had faced were a part of her growth, helping her develop a deeper understanding of faith and the presence of angels in her life.

One evening, as she sat in her favorite spot by the window, she opened her journal and wrote a final entry for the chapter: "Today, I am filled with gratitude for the journey I have been on. The doubts and struggles have taught me that faith is not about never experiencing uncertainty, but about trusting in God's plan and finding strength in my community. I am ready to embrace the future with faith, hope, and the unwavering belief in the presence of my guardian angel."

As she closed her journal, Sarah felt a deep sense of peace and contentment. She knew that her journey of faith was far from over, but she was ready to face whatever challenges lay ahead with faith, hope, and the unwavering belief in the presence of her guardian angel.

With a heart full of gratitude and a spirit filled with faith, Sarah embraced the journey ahead, trusting in the signs and wonders that had become her constant companions. She knew that she was never truly alone and that the divine presence in her life would continue to guide and protect her. The doubts and struggles had brought her this far, and she was ready to continue her journey, knowing that the best was yet to come.

Chapter 9: The Angel's Message

The Vivid Dream

Sarah's journey had been marked by moments of doubt, faith, and divine guidance. Her work at the shelter, the support from the Heavenly Hosts group, and the encouragement of Pastor John had all been vital in helping her navigate the complexities of her mission. However, it was an experience in the form of a vivid dream that would provide her with an unprecedented clarity about her life's purpose.

One night, after a particularly long and exhausting day at the shelter, Sarah went to bed feeling a mix of contentment and fatigue. She had been working with a new influx of guests at the shelter and had faced several challenging situations. As she drifted off to sleep, her mind was filled with thoughts of the people she had helped and the struggles they faced.

In her dream, Sarah found herself standing in a vast, open field bathed in golden sunlight. The sky above was a brilliant blue, and a gentle breeze carried the sweet scent of blooming flowers. The scene was serene and beautiful, a stark contrast to the chaos and hardship she often encountered in her waking life.

As she stood there, taking in the beauty of her surroundings, she noticed a figure approaching her from the distance. The figure was radiant, surrounded by an aura of pure, shimmering light. As it drew closer, Sarah realized that it was an angel, its presence both awe-inspiring and comforting.

The angel had a serene expression, its eyes filled with warmth and compassion. It reached out a hand to Sarah, and she felt an overwhelming sense of peace as she took it. The angel's touch was gentle, and its voice was soft and melodic as it spoke.

"Sarah, you have been chosen for a purpose," the angel said. "Your journey of faith and your work with those in need have been guided by divine hands.

There is more for you to do, and your path is clear. Trust in the guidance you receive and follow the calling of your heart."

The angel's words resonated deeply with Sarah, filling her with a sense of clarity and purpose. She felt the weight of her doubts and uncertainties lift, replaced by a renewed determination to fulfill her mission.

Awakening with a Renewed Sense of Direction

SARAH WOKE UP THE NEXT morning with the memory of the dream vividly etched in her mind. She felt a profound sense of peace and clarity, as if the angel's message had lifted a veil of uncertainty that had been clouding her vision. The warmth and reassurance of the angel's presence lingered, filling her with a renewed sense of direction.

She lay in bed for a moment, reflecting on the dream and the message she had received. The angel's words had been clear and direct, offering her a glimpse of her life's purpose and the path she was meant to follow. The dream felt like a divine confirmation of everything she had been doing and a guiding light for the future.

Sarah got out of bed with a sense of determination she hadn't felt in a long time. She knew that she needed to act on the message she had received and embrace the path laid out for her. Her work at the shelter, the support group, and her mission to help others were all part of a greater plan, and she was ready to fully commit to it.

Strengthening Her Resolve

SARAH SPENT THE MORNING journaling about her dream and the clarity it had brought her. She described the serene field, the radiant angel, and the powerful message she had received. Writing it down helped solidify her resolve and reminded her of the divine presence guiding her journey.

Her journal entry read: "Last night, I had a vivid dream where an angel delivered a clear message about my life's purpose. The angel told me that my journey of faith and my work with those in need have been guided by divine hands. I feel a renewed sense of direction and determination to follow the path laid out for me. I am ready to embrace my mission with faith and trust in divine guidance."

After finishing her entry, Sarah felt a renewed sense of purpose. She decided to visit Pastor John to share her dream and seek his guidance on how to move forward with her mission.

Sharing the Dream with Pastor John

LATER THAT DAY, SARAH met with Pastor John at the church. He greeted her warmly, noticing the determined look in her eyes.

"Sarah, it's good to see you. You look like you have something important to share," he said, inviting her to sit down.

Sarah smiled, feeling the reassurance of the angel's message once more. "I had a vivid dream last night, Pastor John. An angel appeared to me and delivered a clear message about my life's purpose. It was so profound and real, and I feel like I have a renewed sense of direction."

Pastor John listened intently as Sarah recounted the details of her dream. When she finished, he nodded thoughtfully. "It sounds like a powerful experience, Sarah. Dreams can be a significant way for God to communicate with us, especially when they leave such a lasting impression."

"Yes, it felt like a divine confirmation of everything I've been doing," Sarah said. "I want to fully embrace my mission and follow the path laid out for me. But I'm not sure what the next steps should be."

Pastor John smiled, his eyes reflecting a deep understanding. "The first step is to continue trusting in the divine guidance you've received. Your work at the shelter and with the support group has already made a significant impact. Perhaps it's time to expand your reach and find new ways to support those in need."

Expanding Her Mission

INSPIRED BY PASTOR John's words, Sarah began to explore ways to expand her mission and reach even more people. She continued her work at the shelter, but also started looking for opportunities to collaborate with other organizations and create new initiatives that aligned with her calling.

One day, while visiting a community center, Sarah met a woman named Rebecca who ran a program for at-risk youth. Rebecca shared her passion for helping young people overcome the challenges they faced, and Sarah felt an instant connection to her mission.

"We're always looking for volunteers and partners who can provide support and mentorship to our youth," Rebecca said. "It sounds like you have a lot of experience and a strong sense of purpose. Would you be interested in getting involved?"

Sarah felt a surge of excitement. "Yes, I'd love to help. I believe that supporting young people is crucial, and I'd be honored to be a part of your program."

Rebecca smiled, grateful for Sarah's enthusiasm. "That's wonderful. We can always use more mentors who are dedicated to making a difference. Let's discuss how you can get involved and contribute to our efforts."

Mentoring At-Risk Youth

SARAH BEGAN VOLUNTEERING as a mentor at Rebecca's program, working with at-risk youth who were facing various challenges, including homelessness, substance abuse, and family instability. She found that her experiences at the shelter and the support group had prepared her well for this new role.

One of the first young people Sarah worked with was a teenager named Jason. He had been in and out of foster care for most of his life and was struggling with feelings of abandonment and anger. Sarah saw a lot of potential in Jason, but she also recognized the deep pain he carried.

During their first meeting, Sarah approached Jason with a warm smile. "Hi, Jason. I'm Sarah. I'm here to support you and help you navigate whatever challenges you're facing. You're not alone in this."

Jason looked at her skeptically, his guard up. "Why do you care? No one else does."

Sarah's heart ached for him. "I care because I believe in you, Jason. I've seen how tough life can be, but I've also seen how people can overcome incredible challenges with the right support. Let's work together and see what we can achieve."

Over time, Sarah and Jason built a strong bond. She listened to his fears and frustrations, offering guidance and encouragement. The whispers of her guardian angel often provided insights that helped her connect with Jason on a deeper level.

One evening, during a particularly difficult conversation, Jason opened up about his feelings of abandonment. "I don't understand why no one wants me," he said, tears welling up in his eyes. "What's wrong with me?"

Sarah felt the whispers guiding her, offering words of comfort. "Jason, there's nothing wrong with you. You've been through so much, and it's not your fault. Sometimes, people make choices that hurt others, but that doesn't define who you are. You are strong, resilient, and worthy of love and support."

Jason looked at her, his expression softening. "Do you really believe that?"

"I do," Sarah said firmly. "And I want you to believe it too. You have so much potential, Jason. Let's work together to help you realize it."

Finding Purpose in Mentorship

AS SARAH CONTINUED her work with the youth program, she found a deep sense of fulfillment in mentoring young people like Jason. She saw the positive impact her support had on their lives and felt a renewed sense of purpose in her mission.

One day, Rebecca approached Sarah with an exciting opportunity. "We've been awarded a grant to expand our program and offer more resources to our youth. We'd like you to take on a leadership role and help us develop new initiatives. What do you think?"

Sarah was thrilled by the prospect. "I'd be honored, Rebecca. This program means so much to me, and I'm excited to help it grow and reach more young people."

With her new leadership role, Sarah worked closely with Rebecca and the rest of the team to develop initiatives that provided holistic support to the youth. They created workshops on life skills, career development, and emotional well-being, as well as providing mentorship and counseling services.

Sarah's experiences with angelic guidance and her journey of faith became an integral part of her work. She often shared her story with the youth, offering them hope and encouragement. The whispers of her guardian angel continued to guide her, helping her navigate the challenges and opportunities that arose.

Trusting in Divine Guidance

ONE EVENING, AFTER a particularly rewarding day at the youth program, Sarah sat by her window, reflecting on her journey. She felt a profound sense of gratitude for the angelic message she had received in her dream and the clarity it had brought to her life.

As she closed her eyes, she felt the familiar warmth of her guardian angel envelop her. The whispers came, offering reassurance and encouragement. "You are on the right path, Sarah. Trust in the divine guidance you receive and continue to follow your calling."

Sarah smiled, feeling a deep sense of peace and contentment. She knew that her journey was far from over, but she was ready to face whatever challenges lay ahead with faith, hope, and the unwavering belief in the presence of her guardian angel.

Her journal entry that night read: "Today, I am filled with gratitude for the angelic message that has guided my journey. The dream brought clarity and purpose to my life, and I am committed to following the path laid out for me. My work with the youth program has been incredibly fulfilling, and I am grateful for the opportunity to make a difference. I trust in the divine guidance I receive and am ready to embrace the future with faith and determination."

Embracing the Journey Ahead

AS SARAH CONTINUED her mission, she found that the clarity and purpose provided by the angel's message gave her the strength to overcome any obstacles she encountered. Her work at the youth program, the shelter, and the support group all intertwined, creating a powerful network of support for those in need.

One day, while visiting the shelter, Sarah met a young woman named Emily who had recently lost her job and was struggling with depression. Emily was withdrawn and reluctant to engage with anyone, her eyes reflecting a deep sense of hopelessness.

Sarah approached her gently, offering a warm smile. "Hi, Emily. I'm Sarah. Is there anything I can do to help?"

Emily looked up, her expression guarded. "I don't know if anyone can help me," she muttered. "I've lost everything."

Sarah sat down beside her, her heart aching for her pain. "We all go through tough times, Emily. But that doesn't mean we can't find a way forward. There are people here who care about you and want to help. Let's take it one step at a time."

As they talked, Sarah felt the whispers of her guardian angel guiding her. She shared stories of others who had faced similar struggles and found hope and healing. Slowly, Emily began to open up, sharing her fears and frustrations.

Over the next few weeks, Sarah worked closely with Emily, helping her access the resources she needed to find a new job and address her depression. She introduced her to the Heavenly Hosts group, where Emily found a supportive community that embraced her and offered spiritual guidance.

A New Chapter

AS SARAH CONTINUED her mission, she felt a deep sense of fulfillment and purpose. The angelic message she had received in her dream had provided her with the clarity and direction she needed to fully embrace her calling. She was making a difference in the lives of those she helped, and she felt a profound sense of gratitude for the divine guidance that had brought her this far.

One evening, as Sarah sat by her window, she opened her journal and wrote a final entry for the chapter: "Today, I am filled with gratitude for the journey I have been on. The angelic message I received in my dream has guided my path and given me the strength to overcome any obstacles. My work with the youth program, the shelter, and the support group has been incredibly fulfilling, and I am grateful for the opportunity to make a difference. I trust in the divine guidance I receive and am ready to embrace the future with faith and determination."

As she closed her journal, Sarah felt a deep sense of peace and contentment. She knew that her journey of faith was far from over, but she was ready to face whatever challenges lay ahead with faith, hope, and the unwavering belief in the presence of her guardian angel.

With a heart full of gratitude and a spirit filled with faith, Sarah embraced the journey ahead, trusting in the signs and wonders that had become her constant companions. She knew that she was never truly alone and that the divine presence in her life would continue to guide and protect her. The angel's message had brought her this far, and she was ready to continue her journey, knowing that the best was yet to come.

Chapter 10: A Divine Intervention

The Crisis Strikes

Sarah's journey had been marked by a deepening faith and a growing sense of purpose, but she was about to face a challenge that would test her resolve and bring her community together in ways she had never imagined. It began one early autumn morning, as dark clouds gathered ominously over the town, heralding the arrival of an unexpected and severe storm.

The storm struck with unprecedented ferocity, bringing torrential rain, fierce winds, and widespread flooding. Roads were washed out, homes were damaged, and power lines were downed, leaving much of the community in chaos. The local authorities were overwhelmed, struggling to respond to the numerous emergencies and coordinate relief efforts.

As news of the disaster spread, Sarah felt a deep sense of urgency and compassion. She knew that she needed to act quickly to help those affected by the crisis. Her heart ached for the families who had lost their homes, the elderly who were trapped without power, and the children who were frightened and confused. Sarah felt the whispers of her guardian angel, urging her to step forward and lead.

Organizing the Relief Effort

WITH DETERMINATION and a clear sense of purpose, Sarah decided to organize a community-wide relief effort. She reached out to Pastor John and other leaders from the church and community organizations, rallying them to support the initiative. They quickly formed a task force, pooling their resources and expertise to coordinate the response.

At the first meeting of the task force, held in the church's community hall, Sarah outlined the urgent needs and proposed a plan of action. "We need to provide immediate assistance to those affected by the storm," she said. "Food, water, shelter, medical care—these are our top priorities. We also need to organize volunteers to help with clean-up and repairs."

The group was galvanized by Sarah's leadership and her unwavering commitment to helping those in need. They divided responsibilities, with some members focusing on gathering supplies, others coordinating volunteers, and still others managing communications and logistics.

Sarah worked tirelessly, driven by a deep sense of purpose and guided by the whispers of her guardian angel. She reached out to local businesses, asking for donations of food, water, and other essential supplies. She contacted neighboring communities, seeking additional support and resources. The response was overwhelming, as people from all walks of life came together to offer their assistance.

Miraculous Events Unfold

AS THE RELIEF EFFORT gained momentum, miraculous events began to unfold, which many in the community attributed to divine intervention. These events served as powerful reminders of the presence of angels and the importance of faith during times of crisis.

One particularly memorable event occurred when the relief team was running low on bottled water. The storm had contaminated the local water supply, and clean drinking water was desperately needed. Despite their best efforts, the task force was unable to secure enough water to meet the community's needs.

Just as they were about to lose hope, a truck from a neighboring town arrived, loaded with thousands of bottles of water. The driver explained that his company had received a surplus shipment by mistake and had decided to donate it to the relief effort. Sarah and the team were amazed and deeply grateful, recognizing the arrival of the truck as a miraculous and timely answer to their prayers.

Another miraculous event took place at the shelter set up in the church's community hall. The shelter was quickly filling up with families who had been displaced by the storm, and the volunteers were struggling to provide enough food for everyone. As the supplies began to dwindle, Sarah led the volunteers in a prayer, asking for divine assistance.

Within hours, local restaurants and grocery stores began delivering food to the shelter, far exceeding what had been requested. The abundance of donations ensured that everyone at the shelter was well-fed and cared for, and the volunteers were left in awe of the seemingly miraculous provision.

The Community Comes Together

AS THE RELIEF EFFORT continued, the community began to recognize Sarah as a beacon of hope and faith. Her leadership, compassion, and unwavering commitment to helping others inspired those around her. People who had never met before came together, united by a shared sense of purpose and a desire to support one another.

One evening, as Sarah and a group of volunteers were distributing supplies in one of the hardest-hit neighborhoods, an elderly woman named Mrs. Johnson approached her. "Thank you, Sarah," she said, her voice filled with emotion. "You've given us hope during this terrible time. We've all been praying for a miracle, and you've been an answer to those prayers."

Sarah felt a deep sense of humility and gratitude. "I'm just doing what I can to help," she replied. "We're all in this together, and I believe that our faith and our community will see us through."

As word of the relief effort spread, more and more people joined in, offering their time, resources, and support. Local businesses donated supplies, schools organized fundraisers, and individuals from all walks of life volunteered to help with clean-up and repairs. The sense of unity and collective effort was palpable, and it brought a renewed sense of hope and resilience to the community.

Recognizing the Divine Presence

THROUGHOUT THE RELIEF effort, Sarah continued to feel the guidance and reassurance of her guardian angel. The whispers offered her strength and clarity, helping her navigate the challenges and uncertainties that arose. She knew that the miraculous events and the overwhelming support from the community were signs of divine presence and intervention.

One evening, as Sarah sat in the quiet of her home, reflecting on the events of the past weeks, she felt the familiar warmth of her guardian angel envelop her. The whispers came, offering words of encouragement and affirmation. "You are on the right path, Sarah. Your faith and your actions have brought hope and healing to many. Trust in the divine guidance you receive and continue to follow your calling."

Sarah felt tears of gratitude well up in her eyes. She bowed her head in prayer, thanking God for the strength and guidance that had sustained her. "Thank you for your presence and for the angels who have guided me," she whispered. "I am grateful for the opportunity to serve and to make a difference in the lives of others. Please continue to guide me and help me fulfill my purpose."

A Beacon of Hope

AS THE IMMEDIATE CRISIS began to subside and the community started to rebuild, Sarah's role as a leader and beacon of hope became even more evident. Her tireless efforts and unwavering faith had inspired those around her, and many looked to her for guidance and support.

One day, Pastor John approached Sarah with a request. "Sarah, the community has been through so much, and your leadership has been invaluable. We'd like to hold a special service to give thanks for the relief effort and the miraculous events we've witnessed. We'd also like to recognize you for your extraordinary contributions. Would you be willing to speak at the service?"

Sarah was deeply honored by the request. "Of course, Pastor John. It would be a privilege to share my gratitude and to recognize the incredible efforts of everyone involved."

The special service was held on a bright Sunday morning, with the church filled to capacity. The air was filled with a sense of anticipation and gratitude as the congregation gathered to give thanks for the relief effort and the unity that had brought them through the crisis.

Pastor John opened the service with a heartfelt prayer, thanking God for the strength and resilience of the community. He then invited Sarah to speak, acknowledging her leadership and the inspiration she had provided.

Sarah took a deep breath as she stepped to the podium, her heart filled with gratitude and humility. "Thank you, Pastor John, and thank you to everyone who has come together to support our community during this difficult time. It has been an honor to be a part of this relief effort and to witness the incredible generosity and compassion of so many people."

She paused, looking out at the faces of the congregation, many of whom had become dear friends and fellow volunteers. "We have faced a great challenge, but we have also experienced miracles and divine intervention. I believe that our faith and our unity have been the key to overcoming this crisis. We have seen the power of coming together, of supporting one another, and of trusting in God's guidance."

Sarah continued, sharing stories of the miraculous events and the acts of kindness that had defined the relief effort. She spoke about the importance of faith, even in the face of uncertainty, and the need to continue supporting one another as the community rebuilt.

As she concluded her speech, she felt the whispers of her guardian angel, offering reassurance and encouragement. "Let us continue to walk this path together, with faith, hope, and the knowledge that we are never alone. Thank you, and God bless."

The congregation erupted in applause, their hearts filled with gratitude and admiration for Sarah's leadership and the collective effort that had brought them through the crisis.

Moving Forward with Faith

IN THE WEEKS AND MONTHS that followed, the community continued to rebuild, drawing strength from the unity and faith that had sustained them during the storm. Sarah remained deeply involved in the relief effort, working tirelessly to ensure that everyone received the support they needed.

Her work with the youth program, the shelter, and the Heavenly Hosts group also continued, each initiative enriched by the experiences and lessons learned during the crisis. Sarah found that the clarity and purpose provided by the angel's message in her dream had been reaffirmed by the events that had unfolded, strengthening her resolve to follow her calling.

One evening, as Sarah sat by her window, reflecting on the journey she had been on, she felt a deep sense of peace and fulfillment. She opened her journal and began to write: "Today, I am filled with gratitude for the journey I have been on. The crisis we faced brought out the best in our community, and I have witnessed the power of faith, unity, and divine intervention. I am grateful for the guidance and support of my guardian angel, and I am committed to continuing my mission to help others. I trust in the divine plan and am ready to embrace the future with faith and determination."

As she closed her journal, Sarah felt the familiar warmth of her guardian angel envelop her. The whispers came, offering words of encouragement and reassurance. "You have done well, Sarah. Your faith and your actions have made a difference. Continue to trust in the guidance you receive and follow your calling."

A Lasting Impact

AS THE COMMUNITY CONTINUED to heal and rebuild, Sarah's impact was felt in countless ways. The relationships she had built, the lives she had touched, and the unity she had helped foster all contributed to a stronger, more resilient community. Her story and the miraculous events that had unfolded during the crisis became a source of inspiration for many, reinforcing the importance of faith and collective effort.

One day, while visiting a local school to speak to the students about the importance of community and faith, Sarah was approached by a young girl named Emily. "Miss Sarah, I heard about how you helped everyone during the storm," Emily said, her eyes wide with admiration. "I want to be like you when I grow up. How can I help people too?"

Sarah smiled, touched by the girl's sincerity. "You can start by being kind and compassionate to those around you, Emily. Look for ways to help, whether it's volunteering, supporting a friend in need, or simply offering a smile and a kind word. Every act of kindness makes a difference."

Emily nodded eagerly. "I will, Miss Sarah. Thank you for showing us how to be strong and to help others."

Embracing the Journey Ahead

AS SARAH CONTINUED her mission, she felt a deep sense of fulfillment and purpose. The divine intervention she had witnessed during the crisis had reinforced her belief in the power of faith and the presence of angels. She knew that her journey was far from over, but she was ready to face whatever challenges lay ahead with faith, hope, and the unwavering belief in the presence of her guardian angel.

With a heart full of gratitude and a spirit filled with faith, Sarah embraced the journey ahead, trusting in the signs and wonders that had become her constant companions. She knew that she was never truly alone and that the divine presence in her life would continue to guide and protect her. The crisis had brought her this far, and she was ready to continue her journey, knowing that the best was yet to come.

Chapter 11: The Miracle of Forgiveness

Confronting the Past

Sarah's journey of faith had been marked by moments of divine intervention, personal growth, and a deepening commitment to her mission. However, she was about to face one of her most challenging tests yet—an opportunity to confront a painful chapter from her past and embrace the power of forgiveness.

One autumn afternoon, while organizing supplies at the shelter, Sarah received an unexpected phone call. The voice on the other end was hesitant but familiar, causing a wave of old emotions to resurface.

"Sarah, it's Daniel. I know this is unexpected, but I need to talk to you," he said.

Sarah's heart skipped a beat. Daniel had been a close friend years ago, but their friendship had ended abruptly and painfully when he betrayed her trust. The memory of that betrayal had left a deep scar, and she had avoided any contact with him ever since.

"Daniel... I wasn't expecting to hear from you," Sarah replied, her voice tinged with surprise and uncertainty.

"I understand. I wouldn't have called if it wasn't important," Daniel said. "I've been going through a lot lately, and I've been doing some soul-searching. I realize how much I hurt you, and I need to make things right. Can we meet and talk?"

Sarah hesitated, conflicted by a mix of emotions. The wound from Daniel's betrayal was still raw, but her faith and the guidance she had received over the years urged her to consider the possibility of forgiveness. "Okay, Daniel. Let's meet tomorrow afternoon at the park," she finally agreed.

Seeking Guidance

THAT EVENING, SARAH felt a whirlwind of emotions as she prepared for the meeting with Daniel. She sought solace in prayer, asking for strength and guidance. "Dear God, please help me find the strength to face this challenge. I want to forgive, but the pain is still so fresh. Guide me with your wisdom and grace."

As she prayed, Sarah felt the familiar warmth of her guardian angel envelop her. The whispers came, offering words of reassurance and encouragement. "Forgiveness is a path to healing, Sarah. Trust in your faith and allow yourself to embrace the power of forgiveness."

Sarah spent the night reflecting on her journey and the importance of forgiveness in her faith. She knew that holding on to resentment and anger was not in line with the teachings she cherished. The whispers continued to offer guidance, reminding her that forgiveness was not only a gift to the person being forgiven but also a gift to herself—a way to release the burden of past pain and embrace a future filled with peace and healing.

The Meeting at the Park

THE NEXT AFTERNOON, Sarah arrived at the park, her heart pounding with anticipation. The park was a serene oasis, with trees gently swaying in the breeze and the sound of birds singing in the background. It was the perfect setting for a conversation that she hoped would bring closure and healing.

Daniel was already there, sitting on a bench near the pond. He looked older, wearier, and there was a vulnerability in his eyes that Sarah hadn't seen before. As she approached, he stood up, his expression a mix of hope and apprehension.

"Thank you for meeting me, Sarah," Daniel said, his voice sincere. "I know I don't deserve your forgiveness, but I need to say how sorry I am for what I did."

Sarah took a deep breath, feeling the whispers of her guardian angel encouraging her to listen with an open heart. "Daniel, I appreciate you reaching out. It's not easy to face the past, but I'm here to listen."

Daniel began to speak, recounting the events that had led to their falling out. He explained how he had been struggling with his own issues at the time and had made terrible decisions that hurt those around him. He expressed deep remorse for betraying Sarah's trust and acknowledged the pain he had caused.

"I've spent years regretting my actions, Sarah. I've tried to make amends in other areas of my life, but I knew I needed to come back and face what I did to you. I'm truly sorry," Daniel said, his voice filled with emotion.

Sarah listened intently, her own emotions swirling within her. The pain of the past was still there, but she also felt a growing sense of compassion for Daniel. She could see the genuine remorse in his eyes and felt the whispers guiding her towards forgiveness.

"Daniel, I won't pretend that what you did didn't hurt me deeply. It took me a long time to move past that pain," Sarah said, her voice steady but gentle. "But I believe in the power of forgiveness and healing. I'm willing to forgive you, not just for your sake, but for mine as well. Holding on to anger and resentment has only kept me tied to the past."

Daniel's eyes filled with tears of gratitude. "Thank you, Sarah. You have no idea how much this means to me. I know I can't undo the past, but I hope we can both find some peace and move forward."

The Healing Process

FORGIVING DANIEL WAS a significant step for Sarah, but she knew that the healing process would take time. Over the following weeks, they continued to meet and talk, slowly rebuilding a sense of trust and understanding. Sarah found that each conversation brought a sense of closure and healing, helping her to release the lingering pain of the past.

One evening, after a particularly meaningful conversation with Daniel, Sarah returned home and sat by her window, reflecting on the journey of forgiveness. She felt a profound sense of relief and peace, knowing that she had taken an important step towards healing.

Her journal entry that night read: "Today, I forgave someone who hurt me deeply. It wasn't easy, but I felt the guidance of my guardian angel and the strength of my faith leading me towards forgiveness. This act of forgiveness has become a turning point in my spiritual journey, helping me to release the burden of the past and embrace a future filled with peace and healing."

A Turning Point in Her Spiritual Journey

THE ACT OF FORGIVING Daniel became a pivotal moment in Sarah's spiritual journey. It reinforced the importance of faith, compassion, and the power of divine guidance in her life. She felt a renewed sense of purpose and a deeper connection to the teachings of her faith.

One day, while discussing her experience with Pastor John, Sarah shared how forgiveness had transformed her perspective. "Forgiving Daniel wasn't easy, but it was necessary. It's helped me to let go of the past and focus on the present. I feel a deeper sense of peace and connection to my faith."

Pastor John nodded, his eyes reflecting understanding and admiration. "Forgiveness is one of the most powerful acts of faith, Sarah. It's a testament to your strength and your commitment to living according to the teachings of Christ. Your journey is an inspiration to many, and your willingness to forgive is a testament to the power of divine love and grace."

Sarah felt a deep sense of gratitude for the support and guidance she had received. She knew that her journey was far from over, but she was ready to embrace the future with faith, hope, and the unwavering belief in the presence of her guardian angel.

Sharing the Power of Forgiveness

INSPIRED BY HER OWN experience, Sarah felt compelled to share the power of forgiveness with others. She began incorporating discussions on forgiveness into her work at the shelter and the youth program, helping those she served to understand the importance of letting go of past pain and embracing healing.

One afternoon, while leading a support group at the shelter, Sarah shared her story of forgiveness with the group. "Forgiveness is a powerful tool for healing. It's not about condoning the actions of those who hurt us, but about freeing ourselves from the burden of anger and resentment. When we forgive, we allow ourselves to heal and move forward."

The group listened intently, many nodding in agreement. One woman, named Maria, spoke up. "I've been holding on to anger towards my ex-husband for years. It's affected my relationships and my ability to trust others. Hearing your story, Sarah, makes me realize that forgiveness is something I need to work towards."

Sarah offered words of encouragement and support. "It's a journey, Maria. Forgiveness takes time and effort, but it's worth it. Remember, you're not alone in this. We're here to support each other and help each other heal."

The Community Embraces Forgiveness

AS SARAH CONTINUED to share the message of forgiveness, she saw a positive impact within the community. People began to open up about their own struggles with forgiveness and sought ways to heal and move forward. The sense of unity and support that had defined the community's response to the storm was now strengthened by a collective commitment to forgiveness and healing.

One day, while visiting the youth program, Sarah met a young girl named Emily who had been struggling with anger towards her father. Emily's parents had divorced, and she felt abandoned by her father, who had moved away and started a new family.

"Miss Sarah, I don't know how to forgive my dad," Emily said, her voice filled with pain. "He left us, and it hurts so much."

Sarah listened with compassion, understanding the depth of Emily's pain. "Forgiveness is a journey, Emily. It doesn't happen overnight, and it's okay to feel hurt. But holding on to that anger will only hurt you more. Let's work on this together, one step at a time."

Sarah and Emily began meeting regularly, discussing the steps towards forgiveness and the importance of healing. Sarah shared her own experience with Daniel, helping Emily to see that forgiveness was possible, even in the most challenging circumstances.

Over time, Emily began to let go of her anger and find peace. She wrote a letter to her father, expressing her feelings and her desire to move forward. The act of writing the letter was cathartic for Emily, helping her to release the burden of resentment and embrace healing.

A Deeper Connection to Faith

SARAH'S JOURNEY OF forgiveness deepened her connection to her faith and the teachings of Christ. She found that the act of forgiving Daniel had opened her heart to a greater understanding of love, compassion, and divine grace. The whispers of her guardian angel continued to guide her, offering reassurance and encouragement as she navigated this transformative experience.

One evening, while reflecting on her journey, Sarah felt a profound sense of peace and fulfillment. She opened her journal and wrote: "Today, I am filled with gratitude for the journey of forgiveness. It has been a powerful and transformative experience, deepening my connection to my faith and helping me to embrace healing. I am grateful for the guidance of my guardian angel and the support of my community. I trust in the divine plan and am ready to continue my journey with faith and determination."

As she closed her journal, Sarah felt the familiar warmth of her guardian angel envelop her. The whispers came, offering words of encouragement and affirmation. "You have embraced the power of forgiveness, Sarah. Your faith and your actions have brought healing and hope to many. Continue to trust in the guidance you receive and follow your calling."

Embracing the Future with Faith

AS SARAH CONTINUED her mission, she felt a deep sense of fulfillment and purpose. The journey of forgiveness had strengthened her resolve and deepened her connection to her faith. She knew that her journey was far from over, but she was ready to face whatever challenges lay ahead with faith, hope, and the unwavering belief in the presence of her guardian angel.

With a heart full of gratitude and a spirit filled with faith, Sarah embraced the journey ahead, trusting in the signs and wonders that had become her constant companions. She knew that she was never truly alone and that the divine presence in her life would continue to guide and protect her. The miracle of forgiveness had brought her this far, and she was ready to continue her journey, knowing that the best was yet to come.

A Lasting Impact

SARAH'S JOURNEY OF forgiveness had a lasting impact on her community. The message of healing and compassion resonated deeply, inspiring others to embrace forgiveness in their own lives. The sense of unity and collective effort that had defined the community's response to the storm was now enriched by a shared commitment to forgiveness and healing.

One day, while visiting a local community center, Sarah was approached by a woman named Linda who had been deeply affected by her message. "Sarah, I want to thank you for sharing your story of forgiveness. It inspired me to reach out to my estranged sister and begin the process of healing our relationship. Your words gave me the courage to take that step."

Sarah felt a deep sense of gratitude and humility. "Thank you, Linda. I'm so glad to hear that. Forgiveness is a powerful tool for healing, and it's a journey we can all take together."

As Sarah continued her mission, she found that the journey of forgiveness had strengthened her resolve and deepened her connection to her faith. She knew that her journey was far from over, but she was ready to face whatever challenges lay ahead with faith, hope, and the unwavering belief in the presence of her guardian angel.

With a heart full of gratitude and a spirit filled with faith, Sarah embraced the journey ahead, trusting in the signs and wonders that had become her constant companions. She knew that she was never truly alone and that the divine presence in her life would continue to guide and protect her. The miracle of forgiveness had brought her this far, and she was ready to continue her journey, knowing that the best was yet to come.

Chapter 12: Angelic Guidance

Seeking Guidance in Daily Life

Sarah's journey had been filled with remarkable experiences of faith, forgiveness, and divine intervention. As she continued her mission, she felt a growing desire to deepen her connection with her guardian angel and actively seek angelic guidance in her daily decisions and long-term plans. She believed that by aligning her life more closely with divine guidance, she could fulfill her life's mission with greater clarity and purpose.

Sarah began each day with a prayer, asking for the guidance of her guardian angel in all her actions and decisions. She found that starting her day with this intention helped her stay centered and open to the whispers that had become a constant presence in her life.

One morning, while preparing to meet with a new group of volunteers at the shelter, Sarah felt a gentle nudge from her guardian angel. The whispers urged her to pay special attention to a young woman named Rachel, who had recently joined the team. As Sarah observed Rachel throughout the day, she noticed that Rachel seemed hesitant and unsure of herself.

During a break, Sarah approached Rachel with a warm smile. "Hi, Rachel. How are you finding things so far?"

Rachel looked up, her expression a mix of relief and anxiety. "It's a bit overwhelming, to be honest. I've never done anything like this before."

Sarah nodded, understanding the feeling. "I felt the same way when I first started. It can be a lot to take in, but you're not alone. We're all here to support each other. If you ever need help or have questions, don't hesitate to reach out."

Rachel smiled, her shoulders relaxing slightly. "Thank you, Sarah. That means a lot."

Sarah felt the whispers offering reassurance, affirming that her attention to Rachel was the right step. She continued to check in with Rachel over the next few weeks, offering guidance and support. As Rachel grew more confident in her role, she expressed her gratitude to Sarah, highlighting the importance of the angelic nudge that had prompted Sarah to reach out.

A Pilgrimage to a Holy Site

DESPITE THE ONGOING guidance she received, Sarah felt a yearning for a deeper spiritual connection. She decided to embark on a pilgrimage to a holy site, hoping that the journey would provide her with profound insights and strengthen her bond with her guardian angel. After some research and prayer, she chose to visit the Shrine of Our Lady of Guadalupe in Mexico, a place renowned for its spiritual significance and history of miraculous events.

Sarah shared her plans with Pastor John, who offered his blessings and support. "A pilgrimage is a powerful way to seek deeper spiritual connection and guidance, Sarah. I'm sure it will be a transformative experience for you."

With the encouragement of her friends and community, Sarah set out on her pilgrimage. The journey was both physically demanding and spiritually enriching, as she traveled through beautiful landscapes and encountered fellow pilgrims who shared their stories of faith and devotion.

As Sarah approached the Shrine of Our Lady of Guadalupe, she felt a growing sense of anticipation and reverence. The air was filled with the scent of incense, and the sound of hymns and prayers created an atmosphere of profound spirituality. The shrine itself was a stunning sight, with its vibrant colors and intricate architecture, a testament to the deep faith of those who had built and maintained it.

A Profound Spiritual Encounter

SARAH SPENT SEVERAL days at the shrine, participating in prayers, meditations, and services. She found herself deeply moved by the stories of miracles and divine interventions that had taken place there. Each day, she felt her connection to her guardian angel growing stronger, the whispers becoming clearer and more frequent.

On the third day of her pilgrimage, Sarah decided to spend some quiet time in the garden of the shrine, a serene space filled with blooming flowers and shaded by ancient trees. As she walked through the garden, she felt a profound sense of peace and the presence of her guardian angel more strongly than ever before.

Finding a secluded bench, Sarah sat down and closed her eyes, entering a state of deep meditation. She focused on her breath and the gentle whispers of her guardian angel, allowing herself to become fully immersed in the moment. As she meditated, she felt a warm, comforting light envelop her, and the whispers grew clearer, forming distinct words and messages.

"Sarah, you have been chosen for a special purpose," the whispers said. "Your journey of faith, forgiveness, and service has been guided by divine hands. Trust in the guidance you receive and continue to follow your heart. Your mission is to bring hope, healing, and compassion to those in need. Embrace this path with courage and faith."

Tears of gratitude filled Sarah's eyes as she absorbed the messages. She felt a deep sense of affirmation and clarity about her life's mission. The encounter in the garden was a profound spiritual experience that reinforced her commitment to her journey and her belief in the presence of her guardian angel.

Returning with Renewed Purpose

WITH A HEART FULL OF gratitude and a renewed sense of purpose, Sarah returned home from her pilgrimage. She felt a deep connection to her guardian angel and a clear understanding of her life's mission. The whispers had provided her with insights and guidance, helping her to see her path with greater clarity and conviction.

Sarah's first priority upon returning was to share her experiences and the insights she had gained with her community. She organized a special gathering at the church, inviting members of the shelter, the youth program, and the Heavenly Hosts group to come together and hear about her pilgrimage.

On the day of the gathering, the church was filled with people who were eager to hear Sarah's story. Pastor John introduced her, highlighting the significance of her journey and the impact she had already made in the community.

"Sarah has been a beacon of hope and faith for many of us," Pastor John said. "Her journey to the Shrine of Our Lady of Guadalupe is a testament to her dedication to her faith and her mission. Let us open our hearts and minds as she shares her experiences and the guidance she has received."

Sarah stepped up to the podium, her heart filled with gratitude for the support of her community. "Thank you, Pastor John, and thank you all for being here. My pilgrimage to the Shrine of Our Lady of Guadalupe was a profound and transformative experience. I felt a deep connection to my guardian angel and received clear guidance about my life's mission."

She shared the details of her journey, the spiritual encounters she had experienced, and the messages she had received. The congregation listened with rapt attention, many moved to tears by her words.

"I have been guided to continue my work with even greater dedication and compassion," Sarah said. "My mission is to bring hope, healing, and compassion to those in need. I ask for your continued support and prayers as we work together to fulfill this purpose."

The gathering ended with a heartfelt prayer, led by Pastor John, asking for continued guidance and blessings for Sarah and the community. The sense of unity and shared purpose was palpable, and Sarah felt deeply affirmed in her mission.

Implementing the Guidance

WITH THE INSIGHTS AND guidance she had received, Sarah began to implement new initiatives and strengthen existing ones. She worked closely with the shelter, the youth program, and the Heavenly Hosts group, using the guidance from her guardian angel to inform her decisions and actions.

One of the first initiatives Sarah focused on was expanding the mentorship program at the youth center. She felt a strong nudge from her guardian angel to provide more comprehensive support for the young people she worked with, addressing not only their immediate needs but also their long-term goals and aspirations.

Sarah organized a series of workshops and seminars on topics such as career development, financial literacy, and emotional well-being. She also partnered with local businesses and organizations to create internship and job placement opportunities for the youth. The response was overwhelmingly positive, and Sarah saw many young people thriving and finding new hope for their futures.

Another area where Sarah felt guided to focus her efforts was in providing spiritual support and counseling at the shelter. She recognized that many of the guests at the shelter were struggling with not only physical and material challenges but also emotional and spiritual ones. With the help of the whispers, she developed a program that offered counseling, prayer, and meditation sessions, helping the guests find peace and healing.

One evening, while leading a meditation session at the shelter, Sarah felt the presence of her guardian angel more strongly than ever. The whispers offered her words of encouragement and reassurance, affirming that her efforts were making a significant impact.

"You are bringing light into the darkness, Sarah," the whispers said. "Continue to trust in the guidance you receive and know that your work is fulfilling a divine purpose."

Deepening Community Bonds

AS SARAH CONTINUED to follow the guidance of her guardian angel, she saw the bonds within her community grow stronger. People came together with a renewed sense of purpose and commitment to supporting one another. The sense of unity and shared mission that had defined their response to the storm now extended to all aspects of their lives.

One day, while visiting the youth center, Sarah met a young man named David who had recently joined the program. David was quiet and reserved, but Sarah felt a strong nudge from her guardian angel to reach out to him.

"Hi, David. I'm Sarah. How are you finding things so far?" she asked, offering a warm smile.

David looked up, his expression hesitant. "It's okay, I guess. I'm just not sure where I fit in."

Sarah nodded, understanding his uncertainty. "It can be tough to find your place, but you're not alone. We're all here to support each other. If you ever want to talk or need help with anything, I'm here for you."

Over the next few weeks, Sarah made a point of checking in with David regularly. She learned that he had a passion for art but had never had the opportunity to develop his skills. With the guidance of her guardian angel, she organized an art workshop at the youth center, inviting local artists to mentor the young people and provide them with the resources they needed to pursue their creative interests.

The workshop was a resounding success, and Sarah saw David's confidence grow as he began to express himself through his art. He shared his gratitude with Sarah, highlighting the importance of her support and the impact it had on his life.

"Thank you, Sarah. This workshop has been amazing. I never thought I could do something like this," David said, his eyes shining with excitement.

Sarah felt the whispers offering reassurance, affirming that her efforts were making a significant difference. "You have a lot of talent, David. Keep believing in yourself and following your passion."

Embracing the Future with Faith

AS SARAH CONTINUED her mission, she felt a deep sense of fulfillment and purpose. The guidance from her guardian angel had provided her with clarity and direction, helping her to navigate the challenges and opportunities that arose. She knew that her journey was far from over, but she was ready to face whatever lay ahead with faith, hope, and the unwavering belief in the presence of her guardian angel.

One evening, as she sat by her window, reflecting on her journey, she opened her journal and began to write: "Today, I am filled with gratitude for the guidance I have received. The whispers of my guardian angel have provided me with clarity and direction, helping me to fulfill my mission with greater purpose and compassion. I am grateful for the support of my community and the opportunity to make a difference in the lives of those I serve. I trust in the divine plan and am ready to embrace the future with faith and determination."

As she closed her journal, Sarah felt the familiar warmth of her guardian angel envelop her. The whispers came, offering words of encouragement and affirmation. "You are on the right path, Sarah. Your faith and your actions are making a difference. Continue to trust in the guidance you receive and follow your calling."

A Lasting Legacy

SARAH'S JOURNEY OF seeking angelic guidance and following her life's mission had a lasting impact on her community. The initiatives she had implemented, the lives she had touched, and the unity she had helped foster all contributed to a stronger, more resilient community. Her story and the guidance she had received from her guardian angel became a source of inspiration for many, reinforcing the importance of faith, compassion, and divine guidance.

One day, while visiting the community center, Sarah was approached by a young woman named Emily who had been deeply affected by her message. "Sarah, I want to thank you for sharing your story and for the work you've done. It inspired me to seek guidance in my own life and to find ways to help others. Your journey has shown me the power of faith and the importance of following our calling."

Sarah felt a deep sense of gratitude and humility. "Thank you, Emily. I'm so glad to hear that. Seeking guidance and following our calling can be transformative, not just for ourselves but for those around us. Keep trusting in the guidance you receive and know that you are making a difference."

As Sarah continued her mission, she found that the journey of seeking angelic guidance had strengthened her resolve and deepened her connection to her faith. She knew that her journey was far from over, but she was ready to face whatever challenges lay ahead with faith, hope, and the unwavering belief in the presence of her guardian angel.

With a heart full of gratitude and a spirit filled with faith, Sarah embraced the journey ahead, trusting in the signs and wonders that had become her constant companions. She knew that she was never truly alone and that the divine presence in her life would continue to guide and protect her. The guidance she had received had brought her this far, and she was ready to continue her journey, knowing that the best was yet to come.

Chapter 13: Strength in Adversity

The Unexpected Loss

Sarah's journey of faith had been marked by numerous trials and triumphs, but she was about to face one of the most challenging experiences of her life. It began on an ordinary day, as she was going about her work at the shelter, organizing donations and coordinating volunteer activities. Her phone rang, interrupting her thoughts, and she saw the name of her beloved grandmother, Clara, flash on the screen.

"Hi, Grandma," Sarah answered cheerfully. But the voice on the other end was not her grandmother's; it was her aunt, Marion, and the tone was grave.

"Sarah, it's Aunt Marion. I'm so sorry to tell you this, but Grandma passed away this morning."

Sarah felt the world around her shift. Her grandmother had been a cornerstone of her life, a source of unconditional love and wisdom. Clara had always been a pillar of strength and faith, guiding Sarah through many difficult times with her steadfast belief in God's plan.

"I... I can't believe it," Sarah stammered, her mind reeling from the shock. "She seemed so healthy the last time I saw her."

"She went peacefully in her sleep," Marion said gently. "She always spoke so highly of you, Sarah. She loved you dearly."

As the reality of the loss settled in, Sarah felt a profound emptiness and a surge of grief. She had always turned to her grandmother for comfort and guidance, and now she felt lost without her. She knew she needed to lean on her faith and her spiritual community more than ever to navigate this difficult time.

Leaning on Her Spiritual Community

THE NEWS OF CLARA'S passing spread quickly through the community, and Sarah was overwhelmed by the outpouring of support and condolences. The members of the Heavenly Hosts group, the volunteers at the shelter, and her friends from the youth program all rallied around her, offering their love and prayers.

One evening, Pastor John visited Sarah at her home to offer his support. "Sarah, I am so sorry for your loss. Your grandmother was a remarkable woman, and her faith and wisdom have touched many lives. We are all here for you during this difficult time."

Sarah nodded, tears streaming down her face. "Thank you, Pastor John. It's just so hard to believe she's gone. She was always my rock, and I don't know how to move forward without her."

"Grief is a heavy burden to bear," Pastor John said softly. "But remember, you are not alone. Your grandmother's spirit lives on in your heart and in the legacy she left behind. Lean on your faith, and let us support you through this."

The members of the Heavenly Hosts group organized a prayer vigil in honor of Clara, gathering in the church's community hall to offer their condolences and share memories. Sarah felt a deep sense of gratitude for the love and support she received, and the vigil provided her with a moment of solace in the midst of her grief.

As she listened to the heartfelt prayers and stories about her grandmother, Sarah felt the whispers of her guardian angel offering comfort and reassurance. "Your grandmother is at peace, Sarah. Her love and guidance will always be with you. Trust in the strength of your faith and the support of your community."

The Angelic Whispers

IN THE DAYS THAT FOLLOWED, Sarah found herself leaning heavily on the whispers of her guardian angel for support. The whispers had always been a source of guidance and reassurance, but now they became a lifeline, helping her navigate the overwhelming grief and uncertainty she felt.

One evening, as she sat by her window, Sarah closed her eyes and took a deep breath, seeking the comforting presence of her guardian angel. The whispers came, gentle and soothing, offering words of encouragement and strength.

"Grief is a journey, Sarah, and it is natural to feel lost and overwhelmed. Allow yourself to feel the pain, but also remember the love and joy your grandmother brought into your life. She is watching over you, and her spirit will continue to guide you. Trust in the divine plan, and lean on your faith and community for support."

Sarah felt a sense of peace wash over her as she listened to the whispers. She knew that her guardian angel was with her, providing the strength and resilience she needed to face this difficult time.

Finding Strength in Adversity

AS THE WEEKS PASSED, Sarah began to find moments of strength and clarity amidst her grief. She threw herself into her work at the shelter and the youth program, finding solace in helping others and making a difference in their lives. She knew that her grandmother would have wanted her to continue her mission with the same dedication and compassion she had always shown.

One afternoon, while leading a support group at the shelter, Sarah shared her experience of loss with the group. "Grief is a journey that we all must face at some point in our lives. It's a testament to the love we have for those we've lost. My grandmother was a source of strength and wisdom for me, and her passing has been incredibly difficult. But I find comfort in knowing that her spirit lives on in my heart and in the lives she touched."

The group listened with empathy and understanding, many nodding in agreement. One woman, named Linda, spoke up. "Thank you for sharing, Sarah. I've been struggling with the loss of my husband, and your words give me hope. It's comforting to know that we are not alone in our grief."

Sarah offered words of encouragement and support, reminding the group of the importance of leaning on their faith and community during difficult times. She felt a renewed sense of purpose in her mission, knowing that her own journey of grief and healing could provide comfort and guidance to others.

A Visit to the Cemetery

AS PART OF HER JOURNEY towards healing, Sarah decided to visit her grandmother's grave. She felt a deep need to connect with Clara's spirit and to honor her memory in a meaningful way. On a crisp autumn morning, she made her way to the cemetery, carrying a bouquet of Clara's favorite flowers.

The cemetery was a serene and peaceful place, with trees gently swaying in the breeze and the sound of birds singing in the background. Sarah found her grandmother's grave, marked by a simple but elegant headstone, and knelt down to place the flowers.

"Hi, Grandma," Sarah said softly, her voice filled with emotion. "I miss you so much. It's been so hard without you, but I'm trying to stay strong. Your love and wisdom have always guided me, and I know you are watching over me."

As she sat by the grave, Sarah felt the presence of her guardian angel and the comforting whispers that had become a constant source of support. The whispers offered words of reassurance and love, reminding her that her grandmother's spirit was always with her.

"Your grandmother's love and guidance continue to shine through you, Sarah. Trust in the strength of your faith and the support of your community. You are never alone."

Sarah felt tears of gratitude and sadness stream down her face as she listened to the whispers. She took a deep breath and closed her eyes, allowing herself to feel the presence of her grandmother's spirit and the comforting embrace of her guardian angel.

Lessons in Resilience and Trust

THROUGH THE ADVERSITY of her grandmother's passing, Sarah's faith deepened, and she learned valuable lessons about resilience and trust in God. She realized that even in the face of profound loss and pain, her faith provided a source of strength and hope that carried her through.

One evening, while reflecting on her journey, Sarah opened her journal and began to write: "Today, I am filled with gratitude for the strength and resilience I have found in the face of adversity. The loss of my grandmother has been incredibly difficult, but I have learned to lean on my faith and the support of my community. Her love and guidance continue to inspire me, and I am committed to honoring her memory by continuing my mission with compassion and dedication. I trust in the divine plan and am ready to embrace the future with faith and determination."

As she closed her journal, Sarah felt the familiar warmth of her guardian angel envelop her. The whispers came, offering words of encouragement and affirmation. "You have faced great adversity with grace and strength, Sarah. Your faith and your actions have brought healing and hope to many. Continue to trust in the guidance you receive and follow your calling."

Continuing the Mission

SARAH'S JOURNEY OF healing and resilience continued as she dedicated herself to her mission with renewed determination. She found that her experiences of grief and loss had deepened her compassion and empathy, allowing her to connect with others on a profound level.

One day, while visiting the youth center, Sarah met a young girl named Emily who had recently lost her mother. Emily was struggling with overwhelming grief and felt lost without her mother's guidance.

"Miss Sarah, I don't know how to move forward without my mom," Emily said, her voice filled with pain. "It hurts so much, and I feel so alone."

Sarah listened with compassion, understanding the depth of Emily's pain. "I know how hard it is to lose someone you love, Emily. I lost my grandmother recently, and it's been incredibly difficult. But I want you to know that you are not alone. We are here to support you, and your mother's love will always be with you."

Emily nodded, tears streaming down her face. "Thank you, Miss Sarah. It helps to know that I'm not alone."

Sarah continued to offer support and guidance to Emily, helping her navigate her grief and find moments of healing. She organized a support group for the young people at the center who were dealing with loss, providing a safe space for them to share their feelings and find comfort in one another.

Through her work at the shelter and the youth program, Sarah saw the positive impact of her mission and the strength of the community that had rallied around her. She felt a deep sense of fulfillment and purpose, knowing that her journey of faith and resilience was making a difference in the lives of those she served.

Embracing the Future with Faith

AS SARAH CONTINUED her mission, she felt a deep sense of gratitude for the strength and resilience she had found in the face of adversity. The guidance from her guardian angel and the support of her community had provided her with the strength to navigate her grief and to continue her mission with compassion and dedication.

One evening, as she sat by her window, reflecting on her journey, she opened her journal and began to write: "Today, I am filled with gratitude for the lessons I have learned in resilience and trust. The loss of my grandmother has deepened my faith and my commitment to my mission. I am grateful for the support of my community and the guidance of my guardian angel. I trust in the divine plan and am ready to embrace the future with faith and determination."

As she closed her journal, Sarah felt the familiar warmth of her guardian angel envelop her. The whispers came, offering words of encouragement and affirmation. "You have faced great adversity with grace and strength, Sarah. Your faith and your actions have brought healing and hope to many. Continue to trust in the guidance you receive and follow your calling."

A Legacy of Love and Compassion

SARAH'S JOURNEY OF resilience and faith had a lasting impact on her community. The lessons she had learned and the strength she had found in the face of adversity became a source of inspiration for many. Her story and the guidance she had received from her guardian angel reinforced the importance of faith, compassion, and trust in God.

One day, while visiting the community center, Sarah was approached by a young woman named Linda who had been deeply affected by her message. "Sarah, I want to thank you for sharing your story and for the work you've done.

It inspired me to find strength in my own faith and to support others in their journey of healing. Your resilience and compassion have shown me the power of faith and the importance of following our calling."

Sarah felt a deep sense of gratitude and humility. "Thank you, Linda. I'm so glad to hear that. Finding strength in faith and supporting one another is a powerful way to navigate life's challenges. Keep trusting in the guidance you receive and know that you are making a difference."

As Sarah continued her mission, she found that the journey of resilience and faith had strengthened her resolve and deepened her connection to her faith. She knew that her journey was far from over, but she was ready to face whatever challenges lay ahead with faith, hope, and the unwavering belief in the presence of her guardian angel.

With a heart full of gratitude and a spirit filled with faith, Sarah embraced the journey ahead, trusting in the signs and wonders that had become her constant companions. She knew that she was never truly alone and that the divine presence in her life would continue to guide and protect her. The strength she had found in adversity had brought her this far, and she was ready to continue her journey, knowing that the best was yet to come.

Chapter 14: A Community Transformed

The Ripple Effect

Sarah's journey of faith, marked by divine guidance and angelic encounters, had gradually begun to transform not only her own life but also the lives of those around her. The cumulative effects of her unwavering commitment to her mission, coupled with the support of her guardian angel, had created ripples of change throughout her community.

The stories of Sarah's experiences and the miracles she had witnessed spread like wildfire, inspiring many to renew their faith and seek their own encounters with the divine. People from all walks of life began to share their own stories of angelic presence, creating a tapestry of faith and hope that bound the community together.

One afternoon, while visiting the local grocery store, Sarah was approached by an elderly woman named Agnes. Her eyes were filled with gratitude and admiration. "Sarah, I've heard so much about the wonderful things you've been doing. Your faith and the miracles you've witnessed have inspired me to renew my own faith. I've started attending church again and have found a sense of peace I thought I had lost."

Sarah smiled warmly, deeply moved by Agnes's words. "Thank you, Agnes. I'm so glad to hear that. Faith has a way of bringing us together and helping us find strength and hope."

As she continued her shopping, Sarah felt the whispers of her guardian angel, offering words of encouragement and affirmation. "Your faith and actions are making a difference, Sarah. Continue to trust in the guidance you receive and share your light with others."

Stories of Angelic Encounters

THE TRANSFORMATION of the community was evident in the numerous stories of angelic encounters and miracles that began to surface. These stories were shared at church services, community gatherings, and informal conversations, creating a sense of unity and collective faith.

One evening, during a meeting of the Heavenly Hosts group, Linda, the group's leader, shared a particularly moving story. "I recently met a man named Thomas who had experienced a miraculous intervention. He was in a car accident and was trapped in his vehicle. He said that just before he lost consciousness, he saw a figure bathed in light who assured him that help was on the way. When he woke up, the first responders told him that they had received an anonymous call leading them to the scene. Thomas believes it was an angel who saved him."

The group listened with awe and reverence, many moved to tears by the story. Sarah felt a deep sense of gratitude for the divine presence that continued to guide and protect the community.

Another member, Alice, shared her own experience. "I was going through a difficult time after losing my job. One night, I prayed for guidance, feeling lost and hopeless. In my dream, I saw an angel who told me to trust in God's plan and assured me that everything would work out. The next day, I received a job offer out of the blue, one that was even better than the one I had lost. I truly believe it was divine intervention."

These stories, and many others like them, reinforced the community's faith and inspired a renewed sense of hope and purpose. The recognition of angelic presence and divine guidance became a cornerstone of the community's collective spiritual journey.

Becoming a Spiritual Leader

AS THE STORIES OF MIRACLES and divine encounters spread, Sarah found herself increasingly recognized as a local spiritual leader. Her journey of faith, her dedication to helping others, and her openness about her own experiences with angelic guidance made her a beacon of hope and inspiration.

Pastor John, recognizing Sarah's growing influence and the positive impact she was having on the community, approached her with a proposal. "Sarah, your journey and your faith have touched so many lives. I believe it's time for you to take on a more formal role as a spiritual leader in our community. Would you consider leading a new initiative focused on helping others recognize and embrace divine guidance?"

Sarah was both honored and humbled by Pastor John's proposal. "Thank you, Pastor John. I would be honored to take on this role. I believe that helping others connect with their faith and recognize the presence of divine guidance is a powerful way to strengthen our community."

With Pastor John's support, Sarah began to organize a series of workshops and seminars focused on exploring and understanding angelic presence and divine guidance. These events were open to everyone in the community, providing a space for people to share their experiences, learn from one another, and deepen their faith.

The First Workshop

THE FIRST WORKSHOP, titled "Recognizing Divine Guidance," was held in the church's community hall. The room was filled with people eager to learn and share their stories. Sarah began the workshop with a prayer, asking for divine guidance and blessings for everyone present.

"Thank you all for being here," Sarah said, her voice filled with warmth and sincerity. "Today, we will explore the ways in which we can recognize and embrace divine guidance in our lives. Each of us has a unique journey, and our connection to the divine is deeply personal. Let's open our hearts and minds to the possibilities and support one another in this exploration."

Sarah shared her own journey of faith, recounting the angelic encounters and the guidance she had received. She spoke about the importance of prayer, meditation, and being open to the signs and whispers of divine presence.

"Faith is not just about believing in something greater than ourselves," Sarah said. "It's about being open to the guidance and support that is available to us. Our guardian angels are always with us, offering reassurance and direction. We just need to learn to listen and trust."

The workshop included guided meditations, group discussions, and personal reflections. Participants shared their own experiences and insights, creating a rich tapestry of stories that highlighted the diverse ways in which divine guidance could manifest.

One participant, Michael, shared a particularly moving story. "I've always struggled with anxiety and self-doubt. One night, I was feeling particularly low and prayed for help. As I slept, I had a dream in which an angel appeared and told me that I was loved and valued. The next day, I felt a sense of peace and confidence that I hadn't felt in a long time. It was a turning point for me."

Sarah encouraged everyone to keep a journal of their experiences and reflections, reminding them that recognizing divine guidance was an ongoing journey. "Our connection to the divine is always evolving," she said. "By keeping a journal, we can track our progress, reflect on our experiences, and deepen our understanding of our spiritual journey."

The Ripple Effect Continues

AS THE WORKSHOPS AND seminars continued, the ripple effect of Sarah's faith and the angelic presence became even more pronounced. The community grew stronger and more united, with individuals finding new ways to support one another and embrace their faith.

One day, while visiting the youth center, Sarah was approached by a young girl named Emma. Emma had been attending the workshops with her mother and had been deeply inspired by the stories and teachings.

"Miss Sarah, I want to help others recognize divine guidance too," Emma said, her eyes shining with determination. "Can I start a group at school to share what I've learned?"

Sarah felt a surge of pride and admiration for Emma's initiative. "That's a wonderful idea, Emma. I'm sure you will inspire many of your classmates. I'm here to support you in any way I can."

With Sarah's guidance, Emma started a faith-based group at her school, where students could come together to share their experiences and explore their spiritual journeys. The group quickly grew in popularity, creating a positive and supportive environment for young people to deepen their faith.

The impact of Sarah's work extended beyond the workshops and the youth center. Local businesses began to embrace the principles of compassion and community support that Sarah had championed. They organized charity drives, offered resources to those in need, and created spaces for employees to share their spiritual journeys.

A Transformative Event

THE CULMINATION OF the community's transformation came in the form of a large-scale event called "A Day of Faith and Miracles." Organized by Sarah and supported by the church and local organizations, the event was designed to celebrate the power of faith and the impact of divine guidance on their lives.

Held in the town's central park, the event featured guest speakers, workshops, prayer sessions, and a space for people to share their stories of angelic encounters and miracles. The atmosphere was filled with joy, hope, and a profound sense of unity.

Sarah opened the event with a heartfelt speech, reflecting on the journey that had led them to this moment. "Today, we come together to celebrate the incredible power of faith and the ways in which divine guidance has transformed our lives. Each of us has a unique story, and together, we create a tapestry of hope and inspiration. Let us continue to support one another and trust in the guidance we receive."

Throughout the day, people shared their stories, participated in workshops, and connected with others who had experienced similar journeys. The sense of community and collective faith was palpable, creating an environment of love and support.

One of the highlights of the event was a panel discussion featuring individuals who had experienced profound angelic encounters. Sarah moderated the discussion, asking each panelist to share their story and the impact it had on their faith.

One panelist, Janet, shared her experience of receiving a life-saving message from an angel during a medical emergency. "I was in the hospital, facing a critical surgery. I was terrified and felt completely alone. That night, an angel appeared to me in a dream and assured me that everything would be okay.

When I woke up, I felt a sense of peace and confidence. The surgery was successful, and I truly believe that the angel's presence saved my life."

Another panelist, David, spoke about a miraculous recovery from a serious illness. "I was diagnosed with a rare and aggressive form of cancer. The doctors gave me little hope, but I prayed and asked for divine intervention. One night, I felt a warm light surround me, and I knew it was an angelic presence. My recovery was nothing short of a miracle, and I am now cancer-free."

The stories shared during the panel discussion and throughout the event reinforced the power of faith and the presence of divine guidance in their lives. The community left the event feeling inspired, uplifted, and deeply connected to one another.

Embracing a New Role

AS THE EVENT CONCLUDED and the sun set over the park, Sarah reflected on the incredible journey that had led her to this moment. The transformation of her community, fueled by faith and the recognition of angelic presence, had been a testament to the power of divine guidance.

Pastor John approached Sarah, his eyes filled with pride and admiration. "Sarah, you have done something truly remarkable. Your faith and dedication have transformed this community. You have become a spiritual leader, and your impact will be felt for generations to come."

Sarah felt a deep sense of gratitude and humility. "Thank you, Pastor John. I am honored to have been a part of this journey. I will continue to follow the guidance of my guardian angel and do my best to support and inspire others."

With Pastor John's encouragement, Sarah embraced her new role as a local spiritual leader. She continued to organize workshops, lead prayer groups, and provide guidance to those seeking to deepen their faith. Her journey of faith, resilience, and divine guidance had not only transformed her own life but had also created a lasting legacy of hope and inspiration in her community.

Continuing the Journey

AS SARAH LOOKED TO the future, she felt a deep sense of fulfillment and purpose. Her journey of faith had brought her to a place of profound connection with her guardian angel and her community. She knew that her work was far from over, but she was ready to face whatever challenges lay ahead with faith, hope, and the unwavering belief in the presence of divine guidance.

One evening, as she sat by her window, reflecting on the incredible journey she had been on, she opened her journal and began to write: "Today, I am filled with gratitude for the transformation I have witnessed in my community. The power of faith and the presence of divine guidance have brought us together and created a legacy of hope and inspiration. I am honored to be a part of this journey and to support others in their spiritual paths. I trust in the divine plan and am ready to embrace the future with faith and determination."

As she closed her journal, Sarah felt the familiar warmth of her guardian angel envelop her. The whispers came, offering words of encouragement and affirmation. "You have created a lasting impact, Sarah. Your faith and your actions have brought healing and hope to many. Continue to trust in the guidance you receive and follow your calling."

With a heart full of gratitude and a spirit filled with faith, Sarah embraced the journey ahead, trusting in the signs and wonders that had become her constant companions. She knew that she was never truly alone and that the divine presence in her life would continue to guide and protect her. The transformation of her community had brought her this far, and she was ready to continue her journey, knowing that the best was yet to come.

Chapter 15: Whispering Angels

Reflecting on the Journey

As Sarah sat in her favorite spot by the window, watching the sun set over the hills, she felt a profound sense of peace and fulfillment. Her journey had been marked by incredible experiences, divine guidance, and the unwavering presence of her guardian angel. The whispering angels had transformed her life in ways she could never have imagined, guiding her through challenges and inspiring her to help others find their own paths of faith and healing.

Sarah opened her journal, a constant companion throughout her journey, and began to write: "Today, I am filled with gratitude for the journey I have been on. The whispering angels have guided me, comforted me, and provided me with the strength to face every challenge. Their presence has been a source of profound inspiration, and I am deeply thankful for their guidance."

As she wrote, Sarah reflected on the many milestones of her journey. She thought about the early days when she first began to sense the presence of her guardian angel, the miraculous healing of Grace, and the profound spiritual encounters she had experienced during her pilgrimage to the Shrine of Our Lady of Guadalupe. Each of these moments had been a stepping stone, leading her to a deeper understanding of her purpose and the divine plan guiding her life.

The Early Days

SARAH'S JOURNEY HAD begun with a sense of curiosity and a desire to understand the divine presence she felt in her life. The early days were filled with moments of doubt and uncertainty, but also with the thrill of discovering a deeper connection to her faith. The whispering angels had provided her with reassurance and guidance, helping her navigate the complexities of her mission.

She remembered the first time she felt the presence of her guardian angel, a warm and comforting sensation that enveloped her during a moment of deep prayer. The whispers had been gentle and soothing, offering words of encouragement and love. "You are never alone, Sarah. Trust in the guidance you receive and follow your heart."

Those early experiences had set the foundation for her journey, instilling in her a deep sense of trust in the divine plan. As she continued to listen to the whispers, she found herself guided to people and situations that needed her support and compassion. Her work at the shelter and the youth program became avenues for her to share the love and guidance she received, creating a ripple effect of hope and healing.

The Miraculous Healing

ONE OF THE MOST SIGNIFICANT milestones in Sarah's journey was the miraculous healing of Grace. Her dear friend had fallen seriously ill, and Sarah had prayed fervently for her recovery. During a hospital visit, she witnessed what she believed to be an angelic figure in Grace's room, offering comfort and healing.

The experience had been a turning point, reinforcing Sarah's belief in the power of faith and the presence of angels. The whispers had provided her with reassurance, reminding her that divine intervention was always at work. "Trust in the power of your prayers, Sarah. The angels are with you, guiding and protecting those you love."

Grace's recovery had been nothing short of miraculous, and it had strengthened Sarah's resolve to continue her mission. She knew that the angels were always present, offering their guidance and support to those in need. This experience had also inspired her to share her journey with others, helping them recognize and embrace the divine presence in their own lives.

The Pilgrimage to the Shrine

SARAH'S PILGRIMAGE to the Shrine of Our Lady of Guadalupe had been another profound moment in her journey. Seeking a deeper spiritual connection, she had traveled to the holy site, hoping to experience a profound encounter with the divine. The journey had been both physically and spiritually demanding, but it had brought her closer to her guardian angel and provided her with clarity about her life's mission.

During her time at the shrine, Sarah had felt the presence of her guardian angel more strongly than ever before. The whispers had become clearer, offering insights and guidance that helped her understand her purpose. "Your journey of faith has been guided by divine hands, Sarah. Trust in the path that has been laid out for you and continue to follow your heart."

The pilgrimage had reinforced Sarah's commitment to her mission, providing her with the strength and determination to face any challenges that lay ahead. It had also deepened her connection to her faith, helping her understand the importance of listening to the divine whispers and following the guidance she received.

The Transformation of the Community

AS SARAH CONTINUED her mission, she saw the transformative impact of her faith and the whispering angels on her community. Stories of angelic encounters and miracles spread, inspiring many to renew their faith and seek their own connections to the divine. The community became a place of hope and support, bound together by a shared belief in the power of faith and divine guidance.

Sarah's role as a spiritual leader grew, and she found herself increasingly recognized for her dedication and compassion. She organized workshops, led prayer groups, and provided guidance to those seeking to deepen their faith. Her journey had become a beacon of hope for many, and the whispering angels continued to guide her every step of the way.

One particularly memorable event had been the "Day of Faith and Miracles," a large-scale gathering that celebrated the power of faith and the impact of divine guidance on their lives. The event had brought the community together, creating an environment of love and support that reinforced the importance of faith and collective action.

Continuing the Mission

AS SARAH LOOKED TO the future, she felt a deep sense of purpose and determination. The whispering angels had provided her with the strength and guidance to navigate every challenge, and she knew that her journey was far from over. She was committed to continuing her mission with unwavering faith, helping others recognize and embrace the divine presence in their own lives.

One day, while visiting the youth center, Sarah met a young boy named Daniel who had recently lost his father. Daniel was struggling with grief and felt lost without his father's guidance. Sarah saw a reflection of her own journey in Daniel's eyes and felt a strong nudge from her guardian angel to offer her support.

"Hi, Daniel. I'm Sarah. I heard about your father, and I'm so sorry for your loss," she said gently.

Daniel looked up, his eyes filled with sadness. "Thank you, Miss Sarah. It's been really hard without him."

Sarah sat down beside him, offering a comforting presence. "I know how difficult it can be to lose someone you love. I lost my grandmother not too long ago, and it was incredibly painful. But I want you to know that you are not alone. Your father's love and guidance will always be with you, and there are people here who care about you and want to help."

Daniel nodded, tears streaming down his face. "Thank you, Miss Sarah. It helps to know that."

Over the next few weeks, Sarah continued to support Daniel, helping him navigate his grief and find moments of healing. She organized a support group for children who had experienced loss, providing a safe space for them to share their feelings and find comfort in one another.

Through her work at the shelter, the youth program, and the community, Sarah saw the positive impact of her mission and the strength of the bonds that had been formed. The whispering angels continued to guide her, providing the reassurance and strength she needed to face any challenges that lay ahead.

A Message of Hope and Encouragement

AS SARAH REFLECTED on her journey and the profound impact of the whispering angels in her life, she felt a deep sense of gratitude and fulfillment. She knew that her experiences had not only transformed her own life but had also created a lasting legacy of hope and inspiration for others.

In her final journal entry, Sarah wrote: "Today, I am filled with gratitude for the journey I have been on and the guidance I have received from the whispering angels. Their presence has been a constant source of strength and inspiration, helping me navigate every challenge and fulfill my mission with unwavering faith. I am deeply thankful for the support of my community and the opportunity to make a difference in the lives of those I serve. As I continue my journey, I trust in the divine plan and remain open to the whispers of guidance and love."

With a heart full of gratitude and a spirit filled with faith, Sarah embraced the journey ahead, knowing that the whispering angels would continue to guide and protect her. She felt a deep sense of peace, knowing that she was never truly alone and that the divine presence in her life would always be there to offer reassurance and support.

As she closed her journal, Sarah felt the familiar warmth of her guardian angel envelop her. The whispers came, offering words of encouragement and affirmation. "You have created a lasting impact, Sarah. Your faith and your actions have brought healing and hope to many. Continue to trust in the guidance you receive and follow your calling."

Sarah smiled, feeling a deep sense of fulfillment and purpose. She knew that her journey was far from over, but she was ready to face whatever challenges lay ahead with faith, hope, and the unwavering belief in the presence of the whispering angels.

A Closing Message to Readers

IN THE CONCLUDING CHAPTER of her story, Sarah wanted to leave readers with a message of hope and encouragement. She hoped that her journey and the experiences she had shared would inspire others to remain open to the divine whispers in their own lives.

"Dear readers," Sarah wrote, "I hope that my journey has touched your heart and inspired you to seek your own connection to the divine. The whispering angels are always with us, offering guidance and support, even in the most challenging times. Trust in the power of your faith and remain open to the signs and wonders that surround you. Remember that you are never truly alone and that the divine presence is always there to guide and protect you. Embrace your journey with courage and determination, and know that the best is yet to come."

With these words, Sarah closed her journal, feeling a deep sense of peace and fulfillment. She knew that her journey of faith and the guidance of the whispering angels had created a legacy of hope and inspiration that would continue to touch the lives of many.

As she looked out at the setting sun, Sarah felt a profound sense of connection to the divine and a deep trust in the journey ahead. With unwavering faith and the constant presence of the whispering angels, she was ready to embrace the future, knowing that her mission was far from over and that the best was indeed yet to come.

Don't miss out!

Visit the website below and you can sign up to receive emails whenever Gregory Allen Parker publishes a new book. There's no charge and no obligation.

https://books2read.com/r/B-A-SLYZB-OZXAE

BOOKS 2 READ

Connecting independent readers to independent writers.

Did you love *Whispering Angels*? Then you should read *Voices of Faith*[1] by Gregory Allen Parker!

Voices of Faith: Christian Short Stories offers a collection of uplifting tales that explore the transformative power of faith. From a young girl's miracle in a village crisis to a pastor's inspiring dedication, each story highlights themes of hope, redemption, and compassion. Experience the profound impact of belief through miracles, personal trials, and acts of kindness, as diverse characters find strength and purpose in their faith. This anthology is a testament to the enduring power of prayer and the spirit of Christ's love in everyday life.

---

1. https://books2read.com/u/3G18Rr

2. https://books2read.com/u/3G18Rr

About the Author

Pastor Gregory Allen Parker, a graduate of Trinity Theological Seminary, is a devoted pastor and acclaimed author of Christian fiction. With over two decades of ministry experience, his books explore faith's challenges and triumphs, offering readers inspiring and spiritually rich narratives. Celebrated for his compassionate pastoral care and insightful sermons, Pastor Parker's storytelling reflects his deep understanding of Christian values. When not writing or preaching, he enjoys family time, community volunteering, and the outdoors, continuing to inspire and uplift through his faith and craft.

www.ingramcontent.com/pod-product-compliance
Lightning Source LLC
Chambersburg PA
CBHW022145150726

47992CB00002B/768